CHEERLEADERS

#26

TAKING OVER

JENNIFER SARASIN

D1040918

SCHOLASTIC INC.
New York Toronto London Auckland Sydney

ISBN 0-590-40447-4

12 11 10 9 8 7 6 5 4 3 2 1   7 8 9/8 0 1 2/9

Printed in the U.S.A.   01

First Scholastic printing, February 1987

CHEERLEADERS

TAKING OVER

CHEERLEADERS

CHAPTER

1

Jessica Bennett felt a line of perspiration course down her forehead. But she was right in the middle of a double back flip, so she didn't even bother to wipe it away. Champion gymnasts never let a little discomfort get to them. Jessica was no exception.

> "We're the team,
> We're the cream!
> We're gonna work,
> To win our dream!
> Wolves driving fast,
> Comin' on strong!
> Get another basket,
> No, it won't be long!"

Jessica barely caught Sean Dubrow's hands as he came in close to sweep her up on his shoulders. Their timing was rotten today, and they weren't in sequence with Hope Chang and Peter Rayman, who were supposed to be performing the same moves at the same time. Sean swung Jessica in a circle toward Hope, but Jessica couldn't quite reach the other girl's hands. The two girls flailed around for a second, then having no more time, they slid gently to the ground in splits where they joined Olivia Evans and Tara Armstrong, bowing their heads to their knees on their outstretched legs.

"Well, that felt better to me, at least," Tara sighed, pushing her soaking red hair out of her face. "Mrs. Engborg, how was it that time?"

Ardith Engborg, the cheerleaders' tiny blonde coach, sat to one side of the gym, her hands linked behind her neck. "I've seen better splits from bananas, girls."

"Oh, not again! My legs are like rubber bands," Tara complained. She was pouting, but even the frown didn't make her any less beautiful. Tara was gorgeous, no matter what mood she was in.

"And Jessica, I don't know where your head is. If you can't get those herky jumps in the air, then go home and work on them. You look like you're not even trying," the coach growled.

Jessica felt about two inches tall. If there was anyone who tried, tried until she thought her lungs would burst and her limbs would fall apart, it was Jessica.

"Let's do it again," Olivia suggested gamely. As captain of the Tarenton High cheerleaders, it was her job to whip the rest of them into shape. But that was part of her personality, too. She'd been sickly as a child, and had vowed, the day she got up from her hospital bed, that she would never stop working to be the absolute best — the most extraordinary cheerleader, team captain, and spirit of Tarenton High.

Tara gave her a look. "I can't anymore. Mrs. Engborg, could you just *show* us what's wrong? I really think it might help."

"That's an idea." Hope's delicate face was flushed from practice, but she, like Olivia, never said no. As one of the few Chinese-American students at Tarenton, she sometimes felt like an outsider, afraid to make waves. Mostly, she just wanted to do well, to please herself, the others on the team, and of course, her parents, who demanded perfection of her in everything, be it her violin pieces or her cartwheels.

"Yeah, just give us a quick refresher, would you?" Jessica asked the coach, still feeling the sting of her criticism. "I know we could get it right if we had a model to work off of."

Ardith's usually open face tightened. She deliberated a moment, then snapped, "Olivia, as captain I think it's your job to show the squad the finer points of their moves. Go on."

"Well, okay, but. . . ." Olivia looked at her, puzzled. This wasn't like Ardith. "I think I know what you want, but if you'd just do it once. . . ."

Ardith Engborg swallowed hard, then shook her head. "There's sloppiness everywhere here, from all of you. Boys, too. I expect to see crisp turns and rhythms absolutely on the mark, and

3

what do I get?" She strode to the tape recorder and snapped it on. "From the top. And-a one, and-a two. . . ."

The practice session ended on a bleak note. The Regional Cheerleading Competition was only weeks away, and the team was in no shape to perform. In fact, they were in no shape to do much of anything. Tarenton had lost the last four basketball games — and to their poorest competition. The cheerleaders agreed that it was tough — nearly impossible — to yell themselves blue in the face for a group of exceptionally mediocre players. And now, Mrs. Engborg was critical, too. That didn't help.

"I think this deserves a meeting," Olivia said as she stalked out of the gym fifteen minutes later. "Tara, Jessica, you don't have to be home right away, do you? Oh, Hope, I know you do," she continued before the other girls could speak. "But this is crucial. Guys, what about it? What does everyone say to a pizza?"

"Impossible," Jessica said. "I have other plans." A tender smile crossed her face as she thought about the tall, muscular boy who figured in those plans. Patrick Henley. And after practice going so badly, she just had to talk to him. Be with him.

"And I really can't tell my parents I'll miss dinner on such short notice," Hope said. "I'm sorry, Olivia."

"Oh, you two!" Tara swept her red curls into a ponytail and snapped a rubberband around it. "Anyone would think you needed social secretaries to keep track of your schedules. Now, look at Livvy. She always meets Duffy after school, but she's not whining about missing a date. Where is Duffy, anyway?"

Olivia straightened up a little taller. "He's out of town on assignment. His editor sent him to cover a few of the bowl games around the country for the paper." She had been going out with David Douglas Duffy, better known as "3-D," for several months now. He was a sports reporter on *The Tarenton Lighter*, and when he wasn't around, Olivia felt truly lonely. Especially when everyone seemed to be matched up with someone else.

"Oh, well," Tara brushed that off. "Even if he were around, Livvy would cancel. Hope, I know your parents are impossible, but Jessica, for heaven's sake! What's so important that you would let it come in the way of the regionals?"

"Let her off easy, Tara." Sean grinned, his deep brown eyes teasing Jessica. "The girl's in love. You know how that affects the brain cells."

Jessica didn't even blush. She wasn't sure it was love, exactly, but it was something close. "I'll see you guys tomorrow," she smiled, as she ducked into the locker room.

"Well, how about the rest of you? Hope excluded," Olivia demanded. She understood Hope's problem all too well. Her own mother was strict, too, and only in the past year had Olivia been able to stand up to her mother's smothering overprotectiveness. As for Jessica, well, she kind of understood that, too. When she was with Duffy, there just wasn't anything as important as being a couple.

5

"Let's rest it for a night," Peter suggested calmly. "We're doing okay. Mrs. Engborg's just too demanding, that's all. Hope, I'll meet you in the parking lot in ten." They gave each other a special nod, a quiet sign that they were looking forward to being alone, and vanished into their respective locker rooms.

But the squad *wasn't* okay. Olivia knew they were going to have to get better — and fast. And it wasn't that they didn't practice enough. They worked like demons on their routines. Jessica and Hope even told her they *dreamed* about cheering, and Olivia often did that herself. It wasn't that they weren't friends. They were, and Olivia had always thought that counted for something in a squad. With five newcomers, and Olivia as the last bastion of the old guard, it had taken them a while to band together and become a team. Now, they were as close as the old group had ever been. But they were still lousy.

"All right," she said, looking at the others. "Tomorrow. Without question. We need to talk."

Jessica didn't respond when Olivia yelled good-bye to her and Hope in the locker room. There had never been any love lost between Jessica and Olivia, anyway — perhaps because they were both such terrific athletes and were always in competition. Then there was the business of Walt Manners. Olivia and Walt had dated when they were both cheerleaders the year before. Walt had liked Jessica and it had marked her in Olivia's mind as someone not to be entirely trusted. Even though Jessica had never

6

encouraged Walt, and Olivia knew it.

Tonight, as Jessica hastily pulled on her brown cords and soft heather angora turtleneck, she wasn't thinking about past relationships, or the squad, or the regionals, or anything. Just Patrick. And as she ran down the halls and out the front door of Tarenton High, she wondered whether any boy could ever be as exciting to her as Patrick, with his ruffled head of dark hair, chiseled features, and kind, lopsided smile that warmed her like a fire on a freezing night. Her feet started skimming across the ground as soon as she spotted him standing beside his truck, and in a second she was in his arms.

"How'd it go today?" he asked, softly stroking the chestnut hair that peeked out from under her pink wool beret.

"Bad. Well, that's not true, exactly. More like terrible." She shook her head, wondering if she should burden him with her problems now or later. "Hey!" Her gaze fell on the side of the van and she smiled. "This looks wonderful!" She moved around to the other side and examined the bright new lettering that read: H&T's TLC MOVING. And then in smaller letters beneath, WE TAKE YOU WHERE YOU WANT TO GO.

Throughout high school, Patrick had earned money working for his father, who ran Tarenton's trash collecting business. Patrick had his own truck and used to haul trash after school. But when he graduated, he had joined forces with Pres Tilford, the richest kid in town and son of the owner of Tarenton Fabricators, to start this new venture. Pres's father had been furious when he learned his son and heir not only didn't intend to go to college, but also had no intention of following in his father's footsteps. But Pres was doing well despite his family's disapproval.

"Nice paint job, huh?" Patrick grinned, touching one bright red letter. "I told Clarence Torvald I wanted it to read all the way across town, seeing how Pres and I can't afford to advertise."

"This ought to do it," Jessica nodded. Then she stood on tiptoe and reached up to plant a light kiss on Patrick's lips. "Although I tell everyone I know about you."

"That doesn't count," Patrick smiled. "They know you're prejudiced."

"Me? How could you even suggest such a thing?"

They linked hands and he walked her around to the passenger's side, where he gave her lithe body a boost into the seat. It was so great going out with Jessica — nothing like being with Mary Ellen Kirkwood, he thought to himself ruefully. He'd been nuts about Mary Ellen. Nuts, period. It was a good thing she'd graduated and escaped to New York to start up her modeling career. Because if she'd stuck around, he never would have had the chance to get to know Jessica. And Jessica, unlike Mary Ellen, had no problems with being a small-town girl. And no problems at all with falling for the town trash collector. She wasn't stuck up, or hung up, or anything. She was real. And she cared about him. And she was lovely.

"Where to?" she asked, settling back in her

seat as he climbed up beside her. She didn't spend much time at home these days, now that she and Patrick were together. She knew her mother, Abby, and her stepfather, Daniel would really rather spend time alone, without her. And if she did wander in, Daniel would only quiz her on how much money she'd spent that day. It wasn't worth it. She'd much rather be with Patrick. She'd even started keeping the books for the moving business, just so she'd have an excuse to stay out of the house a little more.

"Well, I thought we'd pick up Pres and go over to Benny's for a burger. Then I wanted to run through some stuff with him for the move we're doing on Saturday. You can put the paint job onto the debit side of the account book while we talk."

"Couldn't we eat and then pick him up afterward?" Jessica suggested as Patrick drove out along the icy roads. She liked Pres, but she resented having to share Patrick with him.

"Yeah, I guess. But the man's got an appetite, just the same as you and me. What's the matter? Why so exclusive?"

"Am I?" she laughed, remembering her squad member's comment about how in love she was. But when Patrick had been in the hospital with pneumonia, something had changed inside Jessica. She had lost her father to illness — she wasn't going to lose Patrick. And it was hard now, even though he was perfectly all right, not to be a little overprotective of their relationship at times. Especially when she felt down and just wanted to talk. "It's okay. Pres can come."

Patrick reached over and squeezed her knee. "Glad to hear you say that. Here's the man in question."

He maneuvered the truck around a corner. There, on the next block, standing in front of Johnson's Hardware, was Pres. He was dressed in nothing warmer than his worn suede jacket and alligator boots, and was hopping from one foot to the other, holding three lengths of nylon rope.

"Hey, bud, wanna lift?" Patrick asked, pulling over and putting on his blinker.

"Might be. Although I see you have company. Wouldn't want to be a third wheel. I mean a fifth wheel." He looked at Jessica intently, his usually laughing eyes wary. He was sensitive to her feelings about him, and didn't want to mess things up for Patrick. He knew how it felt, wanting privacy, particularly when a member of the opposite sex was involved.

"That's okay," Jessica said gamely. "Can't let you freeze to death, Pres. I'd feel awful." She opened her door and scooted over on the seat, closer to Patrick, smelling the delicious odor of Castile soap.

"What are you doing out there anyway?" she asked as Pres climbed aboard. "You used to be attached to that car of yours by the steering wheel."

Pres's red Porsche was notorious around Tarenton. But since he'd gone into business with Patrick, he hadn't had time to go speeding up and down the back roads, the way he used to when he was a free and footloose high school senior.

"Well, my baby has rear axle trouble, and until Patrick and I collect on a few more moving jobs, I can't afford to get it out of the shop." He shrugged, staring out the big windshield into the lights of an oncoming car. "I'm just a poor working stiff, like everybody else. When do we eat?" he demanded. "And more important, who's paying?" He looked at Jessica with a funny smile on his face. Patrick had told him that she was always getting flack from her folks about cash flow, and he didn't like to mooch off anyone. But he was broke. Flat, dead, whatever you want to call it, broke.

"I'll treat," Patrick nodded. "Long as you pick up the tab after you get paid next week. I don't know, Mr. Tilford," he chuckled as he pulled the truck into the last space in Benny's parking lot and turned off the ignition. "For a business partner, you're a pretty bad risk. I hope you don't abscond with the funds someday, taking everything that's mine and leaving me destitute."

He was joking, but he put his arm around Jessica protectively. Pres had always been Number One with the Tarenton girls. He had flash and dash and the Tilford name behind him, not to mention a fancy car. Patrick had his truck and his garbage collection business, period.

"I'm a changed man," Pres claimed, raising his arms in protest. "I don't do that stuff anymore. Honest, Jessica," he whispered as he jumped down from the truck and put up his arms to help her down. She smiled at last, and let him help her. And then, as Patrick came around to their side of the truck, she offered each escort a hand and the three of them ran from the parking lot into Benny's.

"Three hot soups to start," Patrick called to the waitress as they grabbed a booth. "And make 'em hot!"

The room was filled with lots of kids from Tarenton and some of the other high schools. There was noise and laughter and good feeling. Jessica, sitting between two of the most attractive guys in the room, couldn't help but think that she was very lucky. If the squad could just get it together in time for the regionals, she'd be luckier still. And if she could somehow work even harder so that she could please the coach, everything would be really wonderful.

"I find myself pulled toward those video games over there," Pres said, getting up as soon as he'd finished eating. "Let me know when you're done." And he was gone before they could nod.

"I think he knows when he's not wanted," Patrick said pointedly. "Seeing as how he doesn't have a lot of quarters to throw around these days."

"Was I really that lousy to him?" Jessica sighed. She stuck her elbows on the table and dropped her head into her hands. "I didn't mean to be. I'm just . . . oh, Patrick, I never feel we get that much time together as it is, and today at practice — "

She was interrupted by the loud sound of male laughter. About six members of the rangy Garrison High basketball team had just pushed through the door of Benny's and were combing the room for familiar faces. There happened to be a booth filled with Garrison kids right behind Patrick and Jessica.

"Hey, all right!" one blond boy yelled across the room. The rest of the guys followed him over and they all tried to pile into the already crowded booth. There was a lot of shuffling and shoving chairs where they didn't fit.

"Too bad those Tarenton losers won't cough up their places," one kid said loudly. Jessica blanched, assuming he must have recognized her from the last basketball game.

"Don't pay any attention," Patrick said.

But Pres had already heard the comment and was on his way over. "Don't worry about that, Jessica," he said. Then he turned and caught the eye of the Garrison kid who had spoken. "I'm sure you weren't conscious of the fact that you might have hurt someone's feelings. If you're ever conscious at all, that is." Pres, quick to anger, never cared much whether there might be one guy against him or seven.

The guy looked straight at Jessica, then sneered at Pres. "Oh, I was conscious, all right. It was those cheerleaders who were zoned out. They couldn't somersault their way out of a wet paper bag."

Jessica looked into her half-finished soup, wishing she could drown in it.

"Pres, let's get out of here," Patrick suggested pointedly. But Pres was spoiling for a fight. He wouldn't budge.

"Oh, come *on*, Pres," Jessica insisted, grabbing his arm and hauling him out of his seat. She

13

was almost in tears, unable to control the flood of emotion that had threatened to burst from her ever since practice ended.

She ran from the restaurant, out into the frigid night, the two boys behind her. It was even colder now than it had been, or at least it felt that way to Jessica. The faces of the others in the squad — Peter, Hope, Sean, Tara, and Olivia — passed before her briefly, and for a moment she was mad at them all for not being here. They were a team, weren't they? A loyal group of friends. They were supposed to stick up for one another, to band together in adversity.

And then she remembered that she had been the first one to say she couldn't go out with them tonight. The tears started, framing her woeful face in two sparkling lines.

"All right, talk to me," Patrick insisted, catching up with her and taking her shoulders.

Jessica made a noise, but no words would come out. "Jessica, what is it?" Pres's voice floated toward them in the darkness. "I used to be a cheerleader in the old days, remember? What's wrong?" he demanded.

"Everything," she exploded. "We're all messing up and nobody seems to care, or else they care too much, and Ardith Engborg hates me, and — " The words spilled out of her, double time.

"Whoa! Just hold it!" Pres cut in. "First of all, about Ardith, she acts that way with all the kids, just to get them to sweat a little more. As for your performances, well, you've been better, but — "

"You see!" Jessica wept, thrusting her head down on Patrick's chest.

"Great tact, man," Patrick hissed at his partner.

"Look. Look at me." Pres whirled her around to face him. "Nothing's so bad it can't be fixed. The six of you are all talented — probably more than last year's squad, if you think about it. The guys are certainly better gymnasts than Walt and I ever were. Your morale is down because the team's been losing a lot. But that has nothing to do with you."

"Right," Jessica sniffed and tried to pull herself together.

"Now my suggestion is — "

"My suggestion is that you let me drop you off at home, Tilford," Patrick said. "This young lady and I have some talking to do. Alone." He felt guilty now, for not seeing how upset Jessica really was.

"Never mind," Pres grinned. "I'll get a ride from some clown here." He pointed back at Benny's. "I think I can handle them. I guess you and I can talk tomorrow, man. See you." He walked off, leaving Patrick and Jessica standing in the parking lot.

She clung to him tightly for a moment, then took a breath and straightened up. "I'm okay now. I just want to be with you."

"No problem," Patrick assured her. And gathering her up in a powerful hug, he ushered her back toward the moving van.

15

CHAPTER

2

Tara stood on her head for a moment and wondered why she wasn't more interesting. Oh, boys found her attractive, and she knew she could easily turn on lots of bubbly personality, but she just wasn't *interesting*. She longed to be the kind of person who'd be quiet and thoughtful for an entire evening, and then come out with a particularly brilliant statement that would make everyone absolutely fall over. She saw herself at the party after the game Saturday night, maybe dressed in a sweeping cape. Then some incredible guy she'd never seen would walk up to her and say, simply but sincerely, "I've been waiting for you."

"Your knees are a little wobbly," she heard a voice say. "Push forward from the hips."

She felt her feet steadied by a strong set of hands, then lifted slightly upward as Sean pulled her body straight.

16

"You know," he said, as she kicked free of his grasp and did a forward roll onto the mat, "you look prettier upside down." He grinned, showing all his teeth, and she frowned, her fantasy crumbled to bits. She sat down solemnly in front of him, trying to look soulful.

"What in the name of — Tara, all the blood must have gone to your head. C'mon back to earth." He swung around to face Tara and grabbed her hands between his. He really liked her, thought she was a dynamite-looking girl, but he wasn't ready to settle down as part of any couple. There was too much to see and do in the world to lock yourself up with just one partner and throw away the key.

Like his dad said, there was a whole sea of fish out there just ready to jump into his arms. His dad ought to know, too. He was Tarenton Fabricator's top salesman, and Sean couldn't remember a weekend his dad didn't have a great date — or two. And he was starting to consider himself a chip off the old block.

"Sean, do you find me . . . interesting?" Tara asked. She looked intently into his eyes, glad for this moment before practice.

"Oh, yeah. Sure." He laughed and arched into a back flip.

"No, really. I want a serious answer."

"Hey, Tara, when it comes to interesting, it's either you or my history book. And I'd rather talk to you than read a book any time." He chuckled and sprang to his feet, leaping into the air in a straddle jump with a whoop, as Hope and Olivia entered the gym. If Tara was going

17

all weird on him, he would have to rethink their relationship.

"You are about as sensitive as a rock," she grumbled. Leave it to Sean to make a joke out of something crucial.

"You two are coming to Benny's after practice, right?" Olivia said. "I think we can clear this thing up if we all pitch in."

"I'll be there," Tara said.

"Count me in," Sean agreed.

"And Peter said he'd come," Hope told her. "Jessica's the only one I haven't spoken to."

At that moment, Jessica walked into the gym. She was pale, her usually open face a mask, her full lips drawn in a tight line. She was dressed in soft gray sweats, with a red leotard underneath. But even the bright color of her clothing didn't brighten her face.

Olivia took one look at her and hesitated. She wanted to ask if anything was wrong, but Jessica seemed so unapproachable, shut up inside herself. "Well. . . ." She cleared her throat. "Let's get into the warmup, anyhow. There are a couple of old cheers I think we should brush up for the game Saturday, because we need all the time we can get to perfect the new ones."

Peter straggled in with Ardith, carrying the tape recorder, and after a brief couple of stretches, declared he was ready to work. Olivia gave them all the rundown of the cheers they'd be doing that afternoon, and then the session started. It was grueling, uncomfortable, difficult, and not terribly rewarding. It seemed that the more they practiced, the worse they got.

The music stopped. "Take a break," their coach declared with a sigh. She looked at each of them in turn. "Could you kids give me an inkling of why any of you went out for cheerleading? I am dumbfounded, really stupefied by all this. Maybe we should just pull out of the regionals." She was testing them, of course. She wanted them all to get up and scream at her. She expected them to take her to task for such a ridiculous suggestion. But nobody did.

"Can you do one thing right? Tara, what happened to that spread eagle? Peter, that flying fish with Hope is incredibly poor. And Olivia, you performed a back handspring better last year when you were brand new with the team. Jessica, Sean, I don't even have words left to tell you that — "

"Criticize!" Jessica burst out, her pale face reddening. "That's all you ever do. Maybe if you were encouraging once in a while, maybe if just once you told us that we'd done well, it would spur us on. It would make us feel we could get better. But you've been so down on us lately, Mrs. Engborg, it's a wonder we can pick our feet up off the mats."

The others looked at her, astounded that she would dare go on like this. But Ardith Engborg didn't slap her down. Nor did she counterattack, which was what she usually did when someone challenged her. She just stood there and watched as Jessica picked up her practice bag and walked out of the gym.

"Does anyone agree with Jessica?" Mrs. Engborg asked quietly. "Because if you do, you can all get out. As far as I'm concerned, practice is over for the day."

"If you'd just *show* us what's the matter," Tara burst out.

Ardith Engborg drew herself up, appearing much taller than her five feet two inches. She walked around in a circle, then closed her eyes, pondering something. Finally, she turned to the remaining five. "I'll consider today a loss. We'll start fresh tomorrow. But I want the six of you to figure out what's wrong — and correct it. Or else we've got trouble. Bad trouble." She left the room quickly.

"What now?" Sean asked.

"Jessica shouldn't have said that, I suppose," Tara sighed. "But she was just being so . . . miserable to us."

"I agree," Olivia nodded, starting for the door. "Listen, you guys round up Jessica. I'm going to talk to our coach. Meet you at Benny's." She neatened her light brown hair as she left the gym and walked the short distance to Mrs. Engborg's office. Today it felt like the last mile.

"Well, what do you want?" the coach asked sharply when Olivia knocked on the side of the open door.

"I want the straight truth," Olivia said bravely. "Let's have it. You think we ought to break up? You think the squad can't do it? Because if you truly believe that, Mrs. Engborg, then we can't go on." She felt her heart beating rapidly as she stood in the doorway. She was close to tears, and yet there was a solid core of steel running the length of her small body.

"You can do it. Without me." Ardith sat heavily in the big swivel chair behind her desk.

"What do you mean?" Olivia demanded. "That's ridiculous."

"I think I've been unfair to you," Ardith continued, as though Olivia hadn't spoken. "I've been putting this off and putting it off and telling myself it didn't matter. But it does, and it shows on you. On your performance and your spirit, and your morale at all those games we've been losing."

"Mrs. Engborg, I don't get it. We always lose a few games. It was never a question of us making or breaking it for Tarenton. After all, the players have a responsibility, too."

"That's right. But I refuse to let the squad fall apart. Our goal is to win every one, and to behave as though we'd won even when we didn't. And that's where you're falling down on the job. You behave as though you expect to lose."

Olivia drew her breath in sharply. "Well, how can we turn that around? What's the matter with us?" she asked. "And why can't you show us what we're doing wrong?"

"Because. . . ." The coach took a deep breath "Because I need to have an operation and I can't do anything physical until I get this taken care of."

"What . . . what is it?" Olivia hardly dared ask.

Ardith shrugged. "My knee. I hurt it in college, running track, years ago. It was a bad injury, but it healed up pretty nicely by itself. Except the doctor told me that as I got older, the scar tissue build-up might get in my way. And

21

it has. I went to see somebody last week, because I've been in considerable pain lately. And taking it out on you," she added with a rueful smile. "So it's time to get the thing fixed."

"Now?" Olivia asked.

The coach nodded.

"But we're in the middle of the school year. Right before regionals. We've got lots of games left. And it takes a while to have an operation and recover." Olivia knew all too well. She'd spent most of her childhood in hospital beds, coping with a heart problem that had cleared up.

"I'll be back," Mrs. Engborg assured her. "Although they won't know until they do the surgery how long I'm going to be off my feet." A brief smile flitted across her face. "If I have to sit around here in a wheelchair and spur you on, I will. No problem. And now, all my cards are on the table. I guess I have been pretty hard on you lately, but for a reason. See, I've been weaning you away. You're too dependent on me, Olivia — all of you. And it's up to you as captain of the squad to get the group out from under my wing so you can fly on your own. The squad needs encouragement, yes. But more than that, it needs the oomph, the daring, the *will* to perform at top capacity. That's on your shoulders. Okay?"

Olivia took a deep breath. "Okay. But I can't promise you a miracle."

"No, Olivia, you can't. And yet," she said more cheerfully, seeing the concerned look on her captain's face, "miracles do happen. See you later." She smiled.

Olivia grabbed Mrs. Engborg's hand and gave

it a pat. "I'm sorry about the operation. That's rotten."

"It'll be okay. No big deal." The coach closed the door quietly behind Olivia, hoping she was right.

As Olivia walked down the hall toward the front door, she desperately hoped that Mrs. Engborg's knee would heal in no time. For all their sakes.

"I'm sorry, but I refuse to become a punching bag," Jessica was saying, waving her arms emphatically in the air. Patrick, seated to one side of her in the midst of Benny's after-school crush, was trying to calm her down, and Tara, on the other side, was busy scribbling on a napkin, figuring out how many hours of practice they had left before the regionals. Pres sat listening intently at the end of the table.

"You went bananas," Sean said critically. "She was dumping on all of us, and you pick up and storm out of the room. Somebody yells at you so you take your toys and go home. Real grown-up, Jessica!"

Hope sighed. "Do you want to quit, Jessica? I mean, that would really be awful, if you did. After all these months of working so hard and everything. I would be really disappointed if you just walked away."

"I couldn't stop now," Peter acknowledged. "I mean, we haven't been so great lately, we all know that. But that doesn't mean we aren't good. We could turn this thing around on Saturday at the game — even help win that game."

23

"Sort of impossible, don't you think," Pres commented. "Deep River's had a fantastic record so far."

"Thanks so much for your support!" Tara said sarcastically. "Now that you're no longer on the squad, I guess you think you have a right to tear us apart."

"Just a minute!" Pres started to defend himself, and then saw Olivia walking briskly toward them, her small form a blur of red and white. She was wearing Tarenton colors today. She hadn't intended it when she got dressed this morning, but it seemed particularly appropriate right now.

"Well, what's the verdict?" Sean asked.

"Did she say anything about my walking out?" Jessica wanted to know.

"And where do we go from here?" Hope demanded. "What are we going to do?"

Olivia told them everything — about the operation and the weaning away, and the fact that they were not only going to have to start performing brilliantly in a way that they hadn't as yet, but they were going to have to do it on their own.

"Hey, that's nothing." Sean chuckled, easing an arm around Tara's shoulders. "We can manage for a week or two without a coach."

"A week or two? Where do you get your medical information, Dubrow? Out of a comic book?" Pres demanded. "Remember when Chuck Maxwell got hurt in that skirmish last season and had to have knee surgery? He was in traction for two months, then he practically had to be airlifted everywhere for a month after that, and finally he got to hobble around on crutches for

24

another six weeks. If you see Ardith Engborg back in school before the end of the semester, I'll buy everybody here a steak dinner at the Manor." The Manor was the fanciest place in town.

"I hope it's not *that* bad!" Hope said.

"You know, you guys are making a big fuss over nothing," Sean said, digging into the bowl of onion rings the waitress had just deposited on their table. "So Coach Engborg is gone for a while — so what? Where does she get off making herself the center of attraction? I mean, we practically run the show, anyhow. We write a lot of the cheers ourselves and design the moves and everything. So a coach is just there because it's school policy. And she sure hasn't been making life easy for us lately. I say, good riddance."

Olivia's face was white with rage by the time he'd finished. "I'd love to see you manage this squad without her," she spat at him between clenched teeth. "I'd love to see you get us organized, make sure our music is right, correct every mistake that six of us are making, and have the backbone to keep us going when we're so tired we want to quit."

"Livvy's absolutely right," Jessica agreed. "We may not see eye to eye with Ardith Engborg, but we need her."

"Badly," Peter nodded.

"You're an idiot, Sean," Tara scoffed. "You really don't appreciate other people at all."

Olivia scowled at him. "We should prepare ourselves not to have Mrs. Engborg around for a while. Knees are tricky. The doctors never know the extent of the damage until the healing process is underway. So in the meantime, I guess I'm in charge of our revamp schedule."

She looked from one to another of her teammates. She'd had a speech prepared, one she had worked on all the way over from school on her bicycle. But now, seeing their eager, expectant faces, all waiting for her words of wisdom, she couldn't remember a single thing she'd intended to tell them. "Well, I think these discussion sessions are helpful. Maybe if we sit down and talk through each routine before we do it, we'll work better together physically. See?"

"Oh, boy. *Mental* cheerleading — just what we need," Sean grumbled.

"And the next step," said Tara pointedly, "is to get rid of negative attitudes like those."

"Hey, I haven't got an attitude," Sean argued. "I just don't think that talking is going to do a whole lot for our handsprings and cartwheels, is all."

"I think you're wrong, Sean," Jessica said quietly. "Talking implies thinking first. Which is exactly what none of us has been doing lately."

"Well-said," Patrick grinned, drawing her closer and working his fingers along the nape of her neck. Then, before she knew what was happening, he kissed her firmly.

Jessica was slightly embarrassed. The others knew about their relationship, of course, and they'd all seen Jessica in Patrick's arms at one time or another. But right in the middle of Benny's, well, his rather passionate kiss seemed out of place. She was just about to break the warm contact of their lips when she heard a vaguely familiar voice say hello.

And then she looked up into Mary Ellen Kirkwood's gorgeous face. Mary Ellen, the famous — or soon to be famous — New York model. Mary Ellen, who had had Patrick wrapped around her little finger until graduation day last year. Not that Jessica had anything to worry about. After all, she and Patrick were together now, and Mary Ellen was a thing of the past. But still.

"I cannot believe my eyes!" Pres stood up to offer Mary Ellen his chair, and she smiled graciously at him. It was that wonderful, sincere model smile she had mastered so perfectly the very first month she started working in New York City. You couldn't tell if it was real and heartfelt — or completely meaningless.

"Mary Ellen!" Olivia jumped from her seat and ran around to her ex-teammate, hugging her impulsively around the neck. It was important to her to see the former captain of the cheerleaders looking so wonderful and stylish. Even though Olivia had no desire at all for the kind of life Mary Ellen had chosen, it gave her a feeling of hope to see her friend succeeding outside of Tarenton. It meant to Olivia that anything was possible — as long as you cared enough to go out and get it.

"Well, how's everything back East?" asked Tara, admiring the older girl's great haircut and stylish clothing. She secretly thought that she could get away with a similar look: the big shirt over tight black pants; the outrageous dangling

27

earrings shaped like pineapples that accentuated the line of Mary Ellen's long, graceful neck; the blonde curls, artfully brushed out to look as though they just spilled everywhere by accident.

"Everything is. . . ." Mary Ellen paused dramatically and looked at everyone except Patrick. "Everything is totally wild. Party all the time, you know," she laughed. "But it's a bit much for a small-town girl sometimes. I need to come back here every so often, just for a little peace and quiet. So when Mrs. Gunderson asked me to buy some runway samples and bring them here, I jumped at the chance. She paid my ticket back here and a little extra. Anyhow," she added more softly, stealing a glance at Pres under her long eyelashes, "Tarenton's home."

Hope had been watching very carefully the looks — or nonlooks — that passed between Mary Ellen and Patrick. She would fully have expected some reaction, some tension between them because of that kiss. Yet Mary Ellen and Patrick seemed so unfazed by the whole thing, as though it were perfectly normal to fly across the country in a day and walk into a restaurant and see the one you used to adore wrapped around somebody else.

"Well, I am delighted, for one, to welcome you home." Pres got up and walked over to Mary Ellen and gave her an even bigger kiss than Patrick had given Jessica. It was intended as a funny gesture, to break the awkward silence at the table, but it became something else very quickly. Pres knew it, Mary Ellen knew it, and everyone else at the table knew it. It was almost as if she had come

28

back to Tarenton, just to stand there in that hamburger joint and get kissed by Preston Tilford III.

Their lips parted and they stared at each other, dumbfounded.

"We're cheering for a game Saturday night, Melon," Olivia said when everyone else was too silent. "You and Pres have to come, okay? Because we're having a real problem and we need all the advice we can get."

"Great," Mary Ellen nodded, her eyes still on Pres.

"Maybe you can be our substitute coach for a while," Peter joked.

Only then did she tear her eyes away. "What are you talking about?"

"Mrs. Engborg is having a knee operation, so we're not sure who's in charge right now," Hope explained. "We guess Livvy is. At least till the regionals."

"Well, I'll be around for two weeks," she said pointedly in Pres's direction. "I'd be happy to do whatever I can. But right now," she told them, "I should get over to Marnie's. Mrs. Gunderson's waiting."

"See you tomorrow? Same time, same station?" Olivia asked.

"You'll see her," Pres promised, ushering Mary Ellen away from the table. "Eventually."

The only one who hadn't said a word to Mary Ellen was Patrick. As he watched that profusion of blonde curls vanish in the crowd, he felt nothing at all. He turned to Jessica and asked if he could get her another Coke. And Jessica, having no idea what else to say, answered yes.

CHAPTER

The snow came down in bales on Saturday. The ice on the lake was completely covered with a foot of the stuff, like swirled vanilla frosting on a cake. In the streets, only car antennae were visible above the mounds of white, like periscopes trying to get a view of the situation.

Sean called Peter about an hour before the game and asked if Peter would give him a ride, since Sean's little car was going nowhere in this weather. Then Olivia called Peter to say she'd just spoken to Mrs. Engborg and found out that the game was definitely on. She'd also called Tara and Hope, and told them to get ready for Peter to pick them up, too. Jessica had a ride with Patrick.

"The players refuse to call the game," she explained to Peter. "They're desperate to take a shot at Deep River, not that *that's* any surprise."

"Yeah, well, they better do a terrific job. Let's

30

hope the competition has frostbite by the time they get to the gym."

Olivia giggled. "Boy, I wish Duffy was around to cover this. It would be one zinger of a story." She sighed, thinking of 3-D's sparkling eyes. It just wasn't fair that he was away when something important was happening. "I'll leave a candle in the window so you can find the house," she laughed, and hung up.

Jessica came in Patrick's truck with Pres and Mary Ellen. Although it was awkward, thanks to the snow they had a lot to talk about.

"There's no way we'll have any audience at all," Jessica moaned.

"Are you kidding?" Pres exclaimed. "Everybody's dying to see Tarenton win one for a change. I think it'll be a great turnout."

"And if not, we'll cheer for you," Mary Ellen said staunchly. "We'll make enough noise for a hundred missing fans, how's that?"

Jessica smiled at her gratefully. If only Mary Ellen wasn't so gorgeous and perfect. Tonight she had on this incredible plaid coat wrapped around her tall, slim form like a cape. It had a matching cowl-neck hood, from which delicate tendrils of blonde hair escaped.

Despite herself, whenever she looked at Mary Ellen, Jessica felt like a total hick. Which, it occurred to her, was pretty funny, considering that both of them came from the same tiny town and were about equally matched in the sophistication game — except that Jessica had never lived in New York City. And Jessica didn't have one extraordinary piece of clothing to her name.

"How're you feeling?" Patrick asked Jessica over the clunk of the windshield wipers as they pulled into the school parking lot. The headlights scanned the clumps of snow, the heavy flecks penetrating the dark like a rain of confetti.

"Pretty good. Our last two rehearsals were a lot better," she confided. They straggled out into the snow, and with Patrick acting as a buffer against the stiff wind, half-ran, half-stumbled to the door. When they got inside, their cheeks red and faces completely wet, Patrick squeezed Jessica's hand for good luck. But this time, she noted, as she nodded to Mary Ellen, he didn't kiss her.

"See you later. Keep your fingers crossed," she whispered to him.

"Don't worry. If those clowns aren't spurred on to action by your cheering," Patrick assured her, "I'll jump down from the stands and toss a few of *them* in the basket."

Jessica raced for the locker room door, nearly colliding with Peter and Hope, who were coming from the other end of the corridor.

"You made it." Jessica smiled, still thinking about Patrick. He was going to sit next to Mary Ellen all through the game. And even though Pres would be on her other side, she was still nervous. She didn't like the idea of looking up from a cheer and seeing them so close together.

Tara and Olivia were already dressed and standing at the mirror together applying make-up. Jessica and Hope took their uniforms out of their practice bags and hurriedly put them on. Jessica loved the feel of the crisp white pleats that fanned out of the short red skirt, the white sweater with the big red T proclaiming to all the world that Tarenton was the best. But tonight, the clothes were just so much fabric. She was too worried about the game and the party afterward to think much about the way she looked.

"Now, have you got that flip-flop routine straight, Hope?" Olivia was saying.

"I'm sure I do." Hope looked at her captain with an indulgent smile.

"You've been over the order three times already," Tara reminded her, expertly French-braiding the front of her lustrous red hair.

"We'll be okay," Jessica said, tying her shoe-lace, then coming over to stand with the other three girls. "If we can just stop worrying."

"I sure hope there's someone there to watch us take the world by storm. Let's go out and see if the team's here yet," Tara suggested. She was hoping to say hi to Ray Elliott before the game. He was a star forward with an incredible pair of piercing blue eyes that, she noticed, were generally focused on her during halftime.

"Now, remember," Olivia told them as they walked to the door, "don't worry about the score. Just keep up your spirit and cheer like your lives depend on it. This is probably the last time Mrs. Engborg's going to be in the stands for a while."

"Good-bye, fairy godmother," Jessica said, so quietly that Hope had to ask her to repeat what she'd said.

"Well, if she'll grant us one last magic wish

before she goes," Tara said fervently as they made their way down the corridor to the gym, "I'm going to ask that we get to wipe up the floor with Deep River."

"Hey, look at that!" Sean cackled. He and Peter were standing outside the gym, peering through a crack in the door, and Mrs. Engborg was standing beside them as the girls approached.

She beamed at her six prodigies and walked over to Olivia to hand her a few notes. "I don't believe that crowd, do you?"

Olivia and Jessica both noted that she was limping a little. Inconsequential as she said this operation was going to be, she was undoubtedly in pain.

"They came to see our death-defying antics," Sean said. "Hope they didn't come to see us get slaughtered," he added under his breath.

Tara kicked his instep, hard.

"Oh, thanks a lot! That's really going to help my performance!" yelped Sean, hopping up and down on his uninjured foot.

"Both of you, stop it!" Olivia commanded. "I want to know how you really feel. Do you think we can do a great job or not?"

"Yes," Sean admitted, seriously for once. "I really think we can. I was just fooling around."

"Well, why don't you save that energy for the court," Mrs. Engborg suggested gently. "I want to see you guys triumph, okay? Now, the team is lining up, so you better get into place. Go on!" She waved her hands impatiently at them, and they hurried out to get into formation.

Jessica was on her way after Hope and Olivia when she stopped and turned, walking slowly back to the coach. "I'm really embarrassed about walking out the other day. And I'm sorry about your operation, too."

"Sorry never won a game," Mrs. Engborg said without changing her expression.

"When is it?" Jessica asked, pointing to her coach's knee.

"Tuesday A.M."

"We'll be there right after school," Jessica promised, starting back down the hall.

"You better not be! You better be at practice," her coach yelled after her. But Mrs. Engborg was touched, and Jessica could tell by her coach's tone of voice that she'd said the right thing.

They heard the basketball coach, Mr. Cooley, starting to call the lineup. The cheerleaders could feel the excitement in the room as the Deep River team took their places. The crowd really wanted to be there. No one would have missed this game if humanly possible.

Olivia waited until the last name had been called, and then she gave the thumbs-up sign to her squad. At an agreed-upon signal, the six of them made a totem of their hands. Jessica's green eyes flashed as they met Hope's, then Tara's, then Sean's and Peter's, and finally, Olivia's. Tonight was *their* night.

They ran onto the court, yelling the victory cheer at the top of their lungs as the crowd urged them on.

"What's the ticket to VICTORY?
It's power, skill, and ENERGY!
We're the best — now, don't say no,
Give us a hand and let us GO!

Down that court, move it on down!
Start the game, let's go to town!
Tarenton's a winner, can't be beat!
Knock their socks right off their feet!

Give it all you got!
Tarenton's hot!
YAY, team! W-I-N!"
W-I-N!"

There was thunderous applause as Hope and Olivia looped into their flying fish poses off Peter and Sean, and the two other girls did handstands. They all came out of their positions into flip-flops and moved quickly to the sidelines.

The Tarenton team got the ball on the top-off and started working it around the court. Ray Elliott scored the first basket. When Deep River took possession, their center stood out of bounds and tried to inbound the ball far down court to a guard standing all by himself under their basket.

But the Tarenton center, Joe Vogel, tipped the ball as it sailed down court. The Deep River power forward dove for the ball, got a hand on it, but lost control. It rolled out of bounds.

"C'mon, guys!" Olivia nodded. From their places on the sidelines, the cheerleaders stomped and clapped as they chanted:

"J-O-E, he's our man!
If he can't do it,
nobody can!
R-A-Y, he's our man!
If he can't do it,
nobody can!"

Ray gave Tara a wink as he took the ball again and zigzagged down the court, evading one Deep River player after another. He went for the lay-up, but as the ball left his hand, one of the Deep River guards bumped his arm. The cheerleaders heard an audible curse, and Coach Cooley grimaced. He had to pull any player who used foul language on the court.

"You're out, Elliott. Replacement!" He called in P.J. Thompson, who, at 6'3" was the tallest kid on the team.

Olivia led the others in the "Heart and Soul" cheer as the players traded.

"We've got soul,
We've got heart!
We've got winners,
From the start!

Show your stuff,
Act real tough,
YAY, Wolves!"

Jessica landed in a perfect split, then did an aerial, finishing exactly at Peter's feet, as she was supposed to. She looked up to see Patrick beaming down at her, and Mary Ellen and Pres on their feet, cheering for all they were worth.

What was it tonight, anyway? What had turned the tide? Maybe it was the attitude of Deep River, who fully expected to walk away with the game. Their team just didn't seem to be trying. Tarenton, on the other hand, was going to fight to the finish. Each basket erased the miserable failures of the last games; each point represented a step forward for the Tarenton players.

Tarenton had a five-point lead before halftime, and Joe upped the score by two just before the buzzer sounded. As the cheerleaders took the floor for their display, the crowd went as wild as the storm that still raged outside. Tarenton was going to win. They were sure of it.

The cheers spilled from the squad effortlessly. The lifts were higher, the placement more perfect, the moves in unison just as they'd practiced. But what they'd never done in rehearsal was give each other the kind of attention and intense concentration they had tonight. For the first time, there was no hanging back, no waiting and watching, no competition to be the most outstanding. They had learned to work together as one, months ago, but now their work paid off. Each cheerleader was a sparkling facet in the jewel of a team tonight, indivisible, united, joined by a will to win and an unsinkable spirit.

Deep River made a few really superb baskets right at the top of the second half, including a frighteningly perfect ally-oop play where the center passed the ball to a guard who was already poised in midair within slam-dunking reach of the hoop. Suddenly the score was tied, and there was a flurry of anxiety among the cheerleaders.

Then Joe got the ball again, and there was no stopping him. He scored one basket, then got the ball right back when Ray stole it at mid-court from the Deep River guard. Joe dribbled from hand to hand, evading his man as he ran then dished the ball off to Ray. Ray looped it up in the air, watching with glee as it rimmed the basket and fell in.

"Let's give them another cheer," Olivia urged.

"Hey, they're doing fine without us," Sean chuckled as he joined in on "Growl, Wolves, Growl!"

When the game wound down for the finish, the score was Tarenton, 59; Deep River, 45. The Wolves played till the clock ran down with a sense that they could do no wrong — and in fact, they couldn't. Everyone in the stands was on his feet at the end, and when Joe dribbled down the court and stopped, making a successful jump shot from half a court away, the sound of the buzzer was nearly drowned out by the explosion of sound from the crowd.

Mary Ellen, Pres, and Patrick didn't let the cheerleaders get out the door. They were all over them, jumping and leaping and laughing, as were the six triumphant squad members themselves.

Mary Ellen was truly impressed. Jessica was such a brilliant gymnast; Hope was light as air whether on the ground or flying; and Tara was the personality kid, brimming with the kind of enthusiasm that reminded Mary Ellen a lot of herself. Peter was intense and responsible; and as for

Sean, well, he was fun to watch — sort of care-free and spontaneous, just the way Pres had been. Livvy seemed to have grown up a lot. She was still a fantastic athlete, of course, but now she had the poise and maturity to go with her talent.

"You've never been better," Patrick exclaimed.

"I know," Jessica agreed, giggling hysterically.

"Hey, we could have read the phone book out there tonight," Peter said modestly. "Those players were dynamite."

Tara, who clearly agreed, had already pushed her way through the crowd surrounding Ray Elliott, and was offering her own congratulations. Ray's way of saying thanks was to sweep her off her feet and ask her to the party. Tara, sweaty and happy, accepted.

"Let's get cleaned up and get out of here," Olivia suggested, starting for the gym door. The others followed, but were suddenly sobered by the glimpse they got of snow drifting up against the first floor hallway window. And more was falling at an incredible rate.

"How are we ever going to get to the party?" Hope moaned. "Pres's house is all the way out at Fable Point."

"I don't think my mom will be awfully disappointed, somehow," Pres shrugged. "But it *is* too bad. Doesn't look like I'm even going to make it home tonight. I guess I could camp out on a crash mat in the gym, huh?" He stared deep into Mary Ellen's blue eyes, as though asking for a reprieve from this terrible solution to his problem.

"Hey, I live right over on Maple Street," Ray Elliott offered. "We could do the party there. I can't promise any great feast at this short notice, but my mom always keeps some extra chips and sodas around."

"I think you better call first," Patrick said. "I can just imagine her face when you show up with twenty of your pals."

"Nah, she's cool," Ray responded in his typical unruffled manner.

As it turned out, there was no other way to have a party. And there were thirty-one, not twenty. Everybody got exactly one soda and two handfuls of chips, but Mrs. Elliott had several huge packages of frozen Mexican hors d'oeuvres that her husband had refused to eat, so she defrosted all of them. Nobody knew what they were eating, but they were too happy to care.

"I just wanted to tell you," said a soft voice behind Jessica, "that your running tumbles are really incredible."

She turned to see Mary Ellen, looking rather shy and in awe of her. "Oh, gee. Thanks." *That's so bright, Jessica. You really sound like a hick now,* she told herself.

"I bet you can do a triple on the full-sized tramp, right?" Mary Ellen asked.

"Yeah. Most of the time." Jessica couldn't believe this. Here she was, talking to this New York City model, for heaven's sake. And this practically famous and beautiful person was praising her!

"Here's your soda, sweetheart," Pres said, grabbing Mary Ellen's arm. "Don't scarf this down. It has to last all night, okay?" He dragged her away, and Jessica was left to her own thoughts.

"There's Mrs. Engborg," Olivia said, spotting her across the room. "We have to go over." She, Hope, and Peter made their way through the crowd, over to their coach, who was sampling the food with a funny smile on her face. She was deep in conversation with a wiry, muscular, balding man wearing a New York Yankees cap.

"Hi! Having fun?" Olivia asked as soon as she saw a break in the discussion.

"Oh, there you are!" Mrs. Engborg took her by the shoulder and brought her closer. "You were all wonderful. Exceptional. I'm truly proud of you."

The man beside her shook a finger in her face. "Don't praise 'em, Ardith. They'll sit back on their haunches and relax."

Hope and Olivia exchanged annoyed glances.

"We're not about to sit down till the end of the term," Peter joked, but he was clearly upset by the man's comment.

"Everybody, this is Sam Akins, a friend of mine," Mrs. Engborg said. "He used to be the coach for the Davenport Little League team a few years ago, before he moved out of state."

"And now I'm back," the man said, scratching his eyebrow. "I had to come back in the middle of an avalanche, too, wouldn't you know?"

42

Jessica and Patrick had wandered over to talk to Coach Engborg, and Tara dragged Ray and Sean over when she saw her friends all together.

"Well, you've got the beginnings of a basketball team there, I'll say that," Sam Akins told them grudgingly. "Boys just need a little prodding so they'll work harder, jump higher. They need the killer spirit, don't you know."

"Well, you can't complain about what we did tonight," Ray Elliot said pointedly.

"After all, we won," Tara pointed out.

"There's winnning," Sam Akins said. "And there's *winning*. If I were in charge, I'd make a few changes around here."

Mrs. Engborg laughed hastily. "Sam's nickname is 'Slammer.' Made so many hits when he was a kid, they had to widen the ball park. Right, Sam?" And then, quickly and gracefully, she dragged him away.

"Whew! He's something," Peter said.

"Talk about positive attitudes!" Sean said.

"He'd be great as an army drill sergeant," Jessica commented.

Olivia frowned, suddenly wondering why the coach had invited this awful man to their celebration party. "Oh, well," she said. "Where's the rest of my Coke anyhow?"

Someone put a cassette into the tape machine, and someone else rolled back the rug. The room was soon a whirling, jumping crowd of dancers. The mood was festive and wonderful.

Except that six cheerleaders knew something was in the air. And they weren't at all sure that they were going to like it.

43

CHAPTER

4

"You're going to have to make up your mind pretty soon, you know." Pres smiled down into Mary Ellen's blue, blue eyes, leaving his hand on her waist. It fit so perfectly there, so neatly.

"That's not fair, Pres." She grinned. "Asking me whether I want to go home when I'm having the best time I've had in months."

"Is that so?" He stopped dancing long enough to put his arms around her and draw her closer.

"Hey, none of that at my house!" Ray Elliott's voice cut into their private moment. Of course, Tara was tucked under his arm just as tightly as Mary Ellen was under Pres's. "Listen, Tilford," Ray continued, "just because you got out of giving this party and stuck it on me is no reason to get smug and act like you own the lady. If she didn't have jet lag so badly, she probably wouldn't even be dancing with you."

"Don't bet on it, Elliott." Pres smiled.

"Hey, look." Ray took Pres aside, pulling him over to a window. "Man, would you do me a favor?"

"Me?" Pres was not known as a good-deed doer. He liked to cultivate a rakish, I-don't-care attitude that made him seem on top of things. It was a cover for the way he really felt, sometimes shy and a little confused about what he wanted out of life.

Ray shrugged. "Yeah, you. Listen, the snow's about stopped, and some of the kids are going to need a ride home. I'd do it, but I'm just about beat. It was a rough game, you know." He reached in his pocket and produced his car keys. "It'd be okay if *you* took Tara home, see. Not Dubrow. I can't trust him as far as I can throw him."

Pres looked at the ceiling. "Ah, c'mon! You want me to take your date home?"

"And then you can take Mary Ellen home. Got it?" He winked, looking over his shoulder at the two girls, who were deep in conversation. "You can bring the wheels back tomorrow."

"Really?" Pres was suddenly interested. Having a car again after being without his Porsche for two weeks would be a real treat.

"Go on; I'm easy."

Ray was a great guy — Pres had never appreciated him enough. "Sure, good buddy. Don't you worry your head about her. I'll see her home safe and sound," he assured Ray.

He pocketed the keys, then walked over to the girls. "You two need a lift home?" he asked casually.

Tara's response was a peal of good-natured laughter. "I can't believe he got *you* to agree to play chauffeur. But the poor boy is bushed. Well, sure, Pres. Let me just get my parka and say good-night to my date — at *his* door."

Mary Ellen's eyes were shining as she took Pres's hand. "I'll be right with you. Just want to say 'bye to a few folks and tell the group how good they were."

"Don't be long," he warned.

Mary Ellen caught Hope and Peter on her way to the bedroom to get her coat, and congratulated them heartily on their cheering. Then she ran into Sean, who, despite having a girl on each arm, was looking rather glum. He looked so preoccupied when she said good-night that she didn't bother to ask what the matter was. She suspected it had something to do with Tara.

Jessica and Olivia were in the middle of a heated discussion about some routine they were working up for the regionals. It was clear that Olivia was enjoying her captain's status tonight more than ever. Mary Ellen waved as she went past them into the bedroom to retrieve her coat. She turned to find the doorway blocked by a very tall, rugged figure. It was Patrick.

"Oh, hi!" He turned red, then white, as he saw she was alone in the room.

"Hi." She stopped, her coat flung over her shoulders, and stared at him. In the past, any chance meeting with Patrick had affected her like a jolt of lightning, making her legs go weak and her heart start pumping. But now, even as

46

she waited for some reaction, she knew she would get none. What they had had been so good while it lasted, but it was over between them.

"You have a good time?" he asked, simply because he was standing there and she was standing there, and it would have been impolite not to make conversation.

"Very."

"And now Tilford's taking you home," he stated, walking past her to get his coat and Jessica's.

"Well, yes. As a matter of fact, he's taking me and Tara home."

"Uh-huh."

"Patrick!" She was suddenly annoyed. Was he questioning her comings and goings? Her life was her own business now.

"What!" he barked right back at her. He didn't know why she was always running home if she had such a great thing going in New York. He had a feeling she was standing back and judging them all, and he didn't like it one bit.

"For heaven's sake! Pres asked if he could drive me home, not marry me! Why are you acting like an overprotective older brother?"

"Because that's the way I feel now. How are you doing, ah, otherwise?" An old love, even though the feelings had changed, was still important to him.

"Not too badly. I have a runway show to do the week after next. And it really looks like this agent may turn out to take me and. . . ." Her voice trailed off. Why was she trying to impress

Patrick, anyway? "But it's really good to be here. I need to see Tarenton every once in a while."

She heard a slight cough behind Patrick, and then realized that other people wanted to come in and get their coats. She took her purse and walked past him, through the door. She smiled at him softly, thinking of times past.

She spotted Pres on the other side of the room and walked toward him, feeling Patrick's eyes on her. Maybe it was just too soon for them to be friends again. Or maybe they never would be. But she wished him well. She hoped that eventually he would be able to wish her the same.

"Ready to brave the elements?" Pres asked cheerily. Tara, standing beside him, was almost invisible under her ski cap and two scarves.

"Ready, yes. Brave, not very," she said thoughtfully. He didn't know what she meant by that, but he sensed that something had happened to her in the past few minutes. But because Tara was with them, he didn't ask questions. Instead, he squeezed her gloved hand. She nodded at him gratefully, and they started off into the white night.

"Now drive slowly, for heaven's sake!" Tara chided from the backseat as Pres put the key in the ignition of Ray's car.

"Right. No beating speed limits tonight, Mr. Tilford," Mary Ellen agreed.

"You girls are real downers, you know that," he teased. "Just the perfect night for turning this dumb car into a sled, too." He looked over at Mary Ellen, and once again, he spotted that slight melancholy. He had seen her every day for years, in every conceivable mood, but somehow he didn't think he'd ever really seen her until the day before yesterday. Sometimes you need distance from people — and from yourself — to understand how you feel about them.

"Great. Just great. I should have stayed in New York," Mary Ellen grinned.

"Ah, New York, where the snow never settles. It just turns into filthy, dirty slush as it falls." Pres well-remembered his one trip east. He'd had a great time, learned a lot about himself. But tonight, he could hardly remember what the city looked like. Even with his eyes on the road, all he could see before him was Mary Ellen Kirkwood. *What* was happening to him? He cleared his throat.

"So, Mary Ellen, tell me all about New York," Tara said earnestly. "I want to hear everything! Where do you live? How much have you been working? Is living there fabulously expensive?"

"Well, it's. . . ." Mary Ellen debated about telling the truth. She wanted to seem glamorous, after all. "It's great," she said lamely. Suddenly, Pres couldn't wait to be alone with her. Just to talk, to find out how she *really* was. This was odd. Pres Tilford, man about town, fast and free. His attitude toward women had always been to love them and stay with them awhile, but never really get involved. He couldn't change now — could he?

A car came toward them on the other side of the road, going much too fast, and Pres grumbled to himself, slowing as he saw the approach of the next set of headlights. Then a pickup that had been following them began to tailgate, and Pres couldn't shake it. It was the perfect invitation to speed up, and any other night he probably would have, but tonight it didn't seem important to play the game. He was a steady, responsible, totally new Pres.

He arrived at Tara's doorstep ten minutes later, and as he shut off the ignition, they saw the porch light go on. Tara's parents were clearly visible at the front window.

"Oh, boy. Guess I should have called earlier." Tara reached for the door handle with a resigned sigh.

"Hope they go gently on you," Pres said.

"Tell them we won the game first," Mary Ellen counseled Tara, who was already starting up the path.

She gave them the high sign, and they waited until they saw the door close behind her. Then Pres turned to his passenger, a tender smile on his face. "Okay, home we go, lady."

Mary Ellen shook her head. "Not yet. Let's go somewhere else first."

He looked at her quizzically. "I thought you models had to get your beauty sleep. And I don't want *your* parents sitting out on the porch in this weather. It's way past midnight, you know."

"Is it?" She squinted at the clock on the dashboard. "Actually, it's ten of one. Hey, what do you think I do when I want to stay out late in New York? Call my parents and get permission?"

"No, guess not." He chuckled to himself.

"What's funny?"

"Oh, it's just that I'm usually the one arguing for staying out a little longer and the girl's the one who wants to get home."

She pursed her lips in the dark. "Does that mean you don't want to spend any more time with me?"

He grabbed her hands and held them hard. "It means just the opposite. I don't want to spoil anything we may have started tonight. It's different between us than it ever was — you feel it, don't you? — and I want it to stay that way. And going off somewhere to neck in Ray Elliott's car, well, it's just a cheap shot."

"Pres." She folded her arms, hugging herself against the cold. "I don't want to neck. I want to talk to you. Hear about you. Tell you things. Start the car, would you? I'm really freezing."

"Okay," he smiled. "Just one time around the lake, then back home. How's that?" He was delighted as he turned the ignition key, because he was right about them. This time, it was something special.

They drove without speaking until they got to Narrow Brook Lake. Silence lay over the blue-white ice as thickly as the mantle of snow that completely covered it. A few flakes drifted down from the overburdened trees, and they shimmered in the moonlight. But then the clouds rolled in again, darkening the sky. Pres pulled over and parked.

"Really something, isn't it?" he whispered.

"Um. Beautiful." She stared straight ahead,

out the windshield. Then, suddenly, she buried her face in her hands. "Oh, how I miss it here!" There was a catch in her voice, as though she were holding back tears.

"Melon, hey! I mean, Mary Ellen," he corrected himself, taking her in his arms. "What's all this about? I thought the city lights really had you hooked. I thought Manhattan was the only island for you."

She gulped, then looked up at him with a funny smile on her face. "Islands are lonely when you're alone on them," she said simply. "I saw Walt a couple of times for dinner — you know, since he's at Columbia — but he has a whole new set of friends, and they're all at school, and I just didn't seem to fit it. And I called Nancy once at Brown. I figured Providence, Rhode Island, is only a train ride away. We promised to visit but we never did — she's just hysterically busy with classes. I'm so homesick sometimes, I could die," she admitted.

"And tonight, at the game, and afterward at the party, I saw everything that's missing in my life. Oh, you know, not that I want high school all over again — I'm past that now, just as you are. But you've found a niche here, Pres. You're . . . at home." She waved her hands hopelessly before her. "I'm a stranger."

Pres reached over and pulled her close. "The city's hard," he agreed. "We all found that out when we went to visit."

"It's harder than that," she whispered into his shoulder. "I came to New York last summer with a few hundred dollars my great-aunt left me, and visions of fame and fortune dancing in my head. So I answered an ad and got two roommates and an apartment in the East Village right over a restaurant. Even the cockroaches think the place is tacky. Not that that keeps them away!

"The hot water's cold, the cold water's rusty. We also have a terrific view of a brick wall from our living room window. Which is Laurie's bedroom. We drew lots for the real bedroom and Bonnie got that. I got the breakfast nook." She laughed a little. "At least living in the breakfast nook gets me in the mood for waitressing."

"You're waiting tables?" Pres asked, drawing back to look at her face in the dim light. "I thought you had all these runway jobs."

"Some. But those don't pay too much. What you really want is print work or commercials, which is totally impossible if you don't have an agent. And the good agencies aren't interested in newcomers unless they have a totally *different* look, you know, like being six feet tall or having a shaved head. Whenever I walk in the door, they groan."

"How can they do that?" Pres demanded indignantly. "You're perfectly gorgeous."

"Thank you." She smiled ruefully. "But gorgeous doesn't count for much these days. They say they've got more cleancut-girl-next-door types than they can shake a stick at. Oh, I've tried everything. I lost weight; I styled my hair; I got the right clothes. But all it gets me is a ten-minute interview with some assistant to an assistant who tells me that maybe he could do something for my career . . . if I'd just go out with him."

"So what do you intend to do?" Pres was sad about his Mary Ellen's disillusionment. She'd been so fresh, so hopeful when she left Tarenton last summer. Even when he saw her last fall, she'd been in great spirits, filled with a sense of challenge and accomplishment and the fact that she was doing exactly what she'd always dreamed of doing. And dreams die hard.

"Do?" she repeated softly. "I wish I had an idea."

"Are you telling me you want to give it up and come home?" Pres asked quietly.

"No." She turned on him angrily. "You know I'm not a quitter. There *has* to be a place for me as a model in New York. I'm convinced of that. It's just going to take me a little longer than I thought." Then she leaned her head back against the seat cushion and sighed. "My mother is always so excited when I call and say I'm coming for a visit. I know she thinks I'm going to stay this time. And I have to admit that when things are really bad, I consider it. Tarenton is so safe — it feels so warm and secure. Just being with you these past few days, Pres, has sort of centered me again. Like nothing I touched in the city is real, but you are." She grabbed his hand and held on tight.

"Then just keep touching," he told her earnestly. "I'm here."

But she was torn. He could see that. She knew she wasn't going to get anywhere in this world

54

by being warm and secure. And Mary Ellen was nothing if not ambitious. She let go of his hand and hugged herself again.

"I'm sick of rattling on this way. For heaven's sakes, Pres, tell me about you. How's the business going? How are you *feeling* these days?"

Pres grinned at her earnestness and her intensity. The city, far from hardening Mary Ellen, had made her compassionate. And though in the past she'd always been too wrapped up in her own plans to take an interest in anyone else's success or failure, now she was really interested. He regaled her with stories of the moving business, but he purposely omitted mentioning Pattrick. He had a feeling that she couldn't take a whole lot more conflicting emotion for one night.

"Well, I really like the work. I meet people, I keep in shape. I make a little money. Of my own. Not my father's."

"That must be important to you," she said. "Sometimes I think it might be as hard to be born rich as it is to be born poor."

Pres was dazzled by her. By her perceptivity, her determination, her willingness to give the other guy — New York City, or modeling, or Pres himself — a second chance. He'd been dazzled by her in the past, but for all the wrong reasons. He'd wanted to be seen with her then because she was beautiful, and the captain of the cheerleaders, and the girl that every guy in Tarenton High wanted to get close to. Now he wanted her just because she was herself.

He turned her face to his and let his mouth follow the curve of her cheek. Quietly, easily, they slipped into each other's arms. Then they just held each other. It was comforting and warming and wonderful to be together like that.

When at last they pulled apart, the dashboard clock read two. "Do you want to take me home now?" she asked him.

"Of course not. I want to stay here with you all night. But they'd find our frozen bodies in the morning, my blue lips glued to yours, and it would be pretty grim. I can see the headlines now: 'Former Cheerleaders Always Stick Together.' "

"Ooh!" She made a face at the pun, then grabbed him impulsively around the head and hugged him. "You're crazy, you know that?"

Crazy about you, he wanted to say. But it was too soon for that. He nodded his agreement, told her to buckle up, and started the car again.

As they kissed one last time in front of the turquoise house that the Kirkwoods called home, nothing mattered except the intensity of their feelings. As they got out of the car, still holding hands, the moon came out from behind a cloud and shone down on them, showing them the way up the path to her house.

CHAPTER

Tara caught up with Sean in the hall right before lunch on Monday, and he didn't say hi. He didn't even nod at her. Instead, he suddenly became very busy checking to see that he still had all his notebooks under his arm.

"Hi," Tara ventured.

"Oh, hello," he said, as though he were seeing her for the first time.

"Did Olivia tell you Mrs. Engborg is bringing that guy to practice this afternoon?" She was being terribly chatty, talking too fast.

Sean scowled at her. "What guy?"

"The one at the party. The drill sergeant. She said she wanted him to see how we work together. Which means we really have to be on top of things."

"Why should I perform for that clown?" Sean was very annoyed, but he wasn't about to let on that she'd gotten to him with her rotten behavior. It wasn't like they dated on a steady basis or

57

anything, but if there was a party after a game, it was sort of understood that they would hang out together — unless one of them had made a prior arrangement and told the other about it.

Tara shrugged. "Anyway, Olivia told me to round up everybody I saw and get them over to our favorite corner table for a strategy session during lunch. Consider yourself rounded up."

"Okay." He quickened his pace, walking briskly ahead of her in the direction of the cafeteria.

Tara made a face. Her parents were furious with her because she'd come home so late on Saturday, and now Sean wouldn't talk to her because she'd spent the whole party with Ray Elliott. Well, it was his own fault. He never made a fuss over her, he was always looking at other girls, and Ray was clearly the hero of the evening. And it wasn't fair. Why did she have to tell Sean in advance that she had a date?

Hope and Peter were already at the table eating their sandwiches, and Sean was seated beside them with his nose in a newspaper when Jessica and Tara got off the lunch line.

"Where's Olivia?" Jessica asked.

"She said she'd be a little late," Hope explained. "She wanted to stop and talk to Coach Engborg alone."

"Say, Pres and Mary Ellen drove me home from the party the other night," Tara said pointedly, so that Sean would know that Ray hadn't brought her home, "and I think something's going on."

"What do you mean?" Hope asked.

58

"Well, I know they used to go out occasionally last year, but it was never anything much. This time, though, well, all I can say is if she weren't living over a thousand miles away, they might actually get serious."

"You're kidding!" Jessica exclaimed. She hated gossip, and rarely even acknowledged the random rumors that were always floating around school, but thanks to Pres and Patrick's business, she prided herself on knowing Pres pretty well. And he was most certainly not a one-woman man.

"No, really," Tara confided. "The boy was positively starry-eyed when he dropped me off. And she looked pretty moony herself." Tara smiled and settled down to the salad and tuna melt on her tray. "Rabbit food again," she sighed. "I wish I had truly skinny genes and could eat a zillion calories a day."

"Sean, where's *your* lunch?" Peter asked, pushing down the edge of the newspaper.

"You usually load up a tray with enough food for three," Jessica teased. "Don't tell me you're on a diet."

"Not hungry," Sean grumbled.

"Oh, for heavens' sake," Tara exclaimed, taking the paper from him and shoving the tuna melt in front of him. "Eat this, will you? I don't want you going all faint on us during today's practice."

He narrowed his eyes at her, and reluctantly took a bite.

"I guess he did have a little appetite after all." Jessica grinned.

By the time the sandwich was gone, a small smile had replaced the scowl on Sean's face.

"Do you want me to get you another?" Tara asked.

"Yeah, that'd be great. I mean, no, I can get it. I mean . . . aw, Tara, for Pete's sake!"

"What's wrong?" she asked sweetly as the others pretended not to listen.

"Sometimes you get me so mad," he admitted. "I really can't stand Ray Elliott."

"Well, I like him a lot," Tara declared, tossing her flame-colored mane of hair over one shoulder. "And he finds me exceptionally interesting. Which you don't."

"I never said — " Sean began, but he stopped when he saw Olivia coming toward them, a worried frown on her face. She looked gravely upset.

"What is it?" Peter asked. "Is it about Mrs. Engborg's knee?"

"In a way, yes. Well, she was cleaning out her desk when I walked into her office," Olivia began, "which got me thinking. And she looked so embarrassed when I called her on it, like I'd caught her with her hand in the cookie jar."

"Why would she clean out her desk if she's only going to be out for a few weeks?" Tara demanded.

"That's what *I* wanted to know," Olivia nodded, absently tearing a napkin to shreds as she spoke. "She said she needed her notes and files and stuff because there were lots of things she was going to take care of from home. And then. . . ." Olivia paused dramatically. "She said her replacement was going to need room for *his* things."

"Who's he?" Peter sounded dismayed.

"Oh, can't you just guess?" Tara wailed. "It's that awful man. She said he was coming to watch us practice today."

"Tear us apart, more likely," Sean scoffed. "Great. That's all we need."

"Maybe he's not that bad," Hope suggested. "Maybe he was just trying to act tough the other night. He could be a really fine person."

The others looked at her in disbelief.

"Nice try, Hope," Peter said, stroking her hand. "But I'm a firm believer in first impressions. And his was *lousy!*"

"Don't jump to conclusions, any of you!" Olivia warned.

"Did Mrs. Engborg tell you why they'd picked Mr. Akins for this job? I mean, if he turns out to be awful, I guess we could go to Mrs. Oetjen and protest," Jessica suggested.

"No way." Olivia stuck her elbows on the table and dropped her head into her hands. "The principal's a friend of his. As a matter of fact, Sam Akins and Mrs. Oetjen went to school together. How do you like that!"

"If you tell me they were cheerleaders together, I'll eat that tray," Sean warned.

"No." Olivia laughed, giving him a friendly poke. "They didn't have male cheerleaders back in those days. And he was too busy playing ball, from what I understand."

She looked around the table at her disheartened squad members. "Hey, so what if Mr. Akins is going to be a substitute coach? We have each other, don't we? We said we'd be able to do it on our own if Mrs. Engborg had to be in the hospital, and we can! We'll just listen to him with one ear and go off and do our own thing after practice is over. He won't make a bit of difference in our standing when we get to the regionals."

She spoke with conviction, trying not to let on that she doubted everything she'd just said. Well, it was silly to worry in advance, Olivia figured, starting on her lunch. Anyway, she'd have plenty of time to worry later on.

When the bell rang for the end of English, Jessica and Tara headed straight for the lockers to change. They were both quiet and pensive. Jessica was thinking that if there was any day she should have called in sick for practice and ridden the garbage truck with Patrick, it was today; Tara was wondering whether it would be all right to date both Ray and Sean at the same time. In silence, they put on leotards and sweat pants and light aerobics shoes, then grabbed kneepads and went out into the gym to warm up. They were in the middle of some two-person stretches when the gym door opened and Mrs. Engborg walked in with Sam Atkins.

"We generally start with floor stretches on the mats," she was saying to him. "And then go on to the minitramp. I like to get them precision-perfect on their aerial work before we do the cheers themselves. And then the captain of the group, Olivia Evans, goes through the roster of routines."

"Right."

Olivia heard her name mentioned as she came through the door, and she perked up. She was *captain*, after all, and that gave her a certain amount of say in what went on with her squad, regardless of what any substitute coach might do.

"Oh, good. Olivia!" Mrs. Engborg called. "Come here a minute. You've met, but I might as well introduce — "

"Let's ditch the formalities, Ardith," Sam Akins stated flatly, "and get to work."

Hope, Peter, and Sean heard this last comment as they entered the gym, and their spirits sank. They walked over to the others and immediately began warming up. It was not going to be pleasant.

"All right, folks," Mrs. Engborg said, "while I'm away, as I guess you've heard, Sam Akins will be taking over for me."

"Slammer," he corrected her. "I like the kids to call me Slammer."

Sean muttered something, but he was sitting on the floor with his head on his outstretched legs, so the rude comment was inaudible.

"I've filled him in on the way we work," Mrs. Engborg went on, "and I'm going to let Olivia set and rehearse the routines. I know this change is going to be profitable for all of us. It's always good to have some fresh blood, fresh opinions."

"And I'm not shy about giving opinions, either," Slammer said. He flexed his hands be-

63

hind his head and did a little running in place. "You, over there," he said, pointing at Jessica, "can't you get that leg any higher?"

Jessica was going to tell him that she could get it a lot higher, but not right at the beginning of a workout. She was also going to tell him not to call her "you," but she didn't. She stared right through him and went on stretching.

"Now I want you all to pay attention to Slammer's criticism and use it well. He has a wonderful eye for detail," Mrs. Engborg was saying. "Even if he can seem a little callous sometimes." She grinned.

"Okay, kids." Slammer got down on his haunches and motioned for them to gather around him. "We've got a job to do, and we have to get in shape fast. There are a lot of terrific teams going to Lembrook for the regionals — I've seen a few of them, and there are some real athletes to beat around the district."

"We have a few real athletes among us, too," Sean said evenly. Olivia gave him a warning look. She knew the quiet tone of voice that came just before one of Sean's blowups.

"Yeah, but from what I saw the other night, you're holding back. You've got a lot more to give. I'm going to wrench it out of you. I'm going to make you give and give and give until you think you haven't got a thing left — and then I'll make you give some more.

"Now let's dig in our heels, okay?" Slammer jumped to his feet. "Starting with twenty laps around the gym, then eight sets of jumping jacks. On your marks, and let's go! Hey, hey, run those

64

legs off! C'mon, kids!" Slammer started moving, and unbelieving, the six cheerleaders fell in behind him. Why didn't Mrs. Engborg stop him? they all wondered. But she was sitting quietly on the sidelines, holding her knee.

"You can *beat* those other schools," Slammer yelled above the pounding of feet. "You've got to beat 'em all. While I'm in charge, I want complete attention, and I want a lot of sweat. Understood?" He puffed out each word as he picked up the pace. They were now racing around the gym.

Olivia was furious about this, but she hadn't given up. Suddenly she had a flash of the six of them, wearing their red and white uniforms, standing up with pride on the stage in Lembrook. They were a group, banding together. They had their cheers down pat, and they had the spirit and energy to deliver. Despite this man and his idiotic tactics, they could win! She was certain of it.

"And now, jumping jacks! Okay, line up in back of me, and let's go!" Slammer's face and balding head were bright crimson, but he didn't stop. After the jumping jacks came push-ups, and after those came a series of fast forward rolls that left them all breathless. When he finally called a halt and asked Olivia for the roster of cheers, she could barely speak.

"Cat got your tongue?" he barked at her. "You need more stamina than this, girl. You have to get those cheers out to the last seat in the last row in the house. That's a big auditorium you have to fill. Okay, try it again. And smile this time!"

The man was manic, there was no question about it. He stopped each cheer they started, rearranging them, speeding them up, yelling directions until they were all confused and demoralized.

And then Hope sat down. Peter immediately sat down beside her.

"What's this about?" Slammer asked impatiently.

"I need to rest a second," Hope explained, pushing her sweat-soaked hair out of her face.

"Me, too," Peter chimed in.

"We all do," Sean said. "Look, mister, we don't work this way." Again, his tone was polite, but barely. Mrs. Engborg quickly got up and came over to the group.

"Olivia," she suggested, "why don't you show Slammer that new cheer we're working on for the finale. Sam, this is a real showstopper. The point of it is rhythm and buildup. It's pretty tricky, too, because part of it is syncopated. Okay, Olivia, put everyone in place."

Olivia nodded. The "Sharp" cheer had been the creation of a long winter's afternoon. The six of them had written and choreographed it together, and no one at Tarenton knew a thing about it. The cheer, designed just for the regionals, was their *pièce de résistance*, the capper to what they hoped would be a spectacular performance. And it was hard.

"Places, everybody!" Olivia took center stage and the others lined up behind her. "And, let's go!"

"Make it sharp!
Make it quick!
Dynamite!
Do it right!
Make it stick!

Like a shot,
From a gun!
Speed! Power!
Lightning!
Now we've won!

Tarenton Wolves!
Yay, team!"

The cheer involved a series of split-second daredevil moves, with Olivia and Hope airborne throughout the entire number. The two boys and the other two girls were springboards for the smaller girls' acrobatics, but at the same time, they managed to fit in a variety of thigh stands, jumps, rolls, and cartwheels. The six of them moved so fast, it was almost impossible to tell who was doing what, and the effect was stunning. The cheer was so good they repeated it three times over in different positions on the floor, and each time the cheer went faster.

When they ended, in a circle facing out doing splits, Mrs. Engborg burst into spontaneous applause. "That is the best you've ever done it!" she said. "Now the only trick is keeping yourself fresh enough through the rest of your performance so you won't be too tired to do this one just right."

"Ardith, I want to make a small suggestion," Slammer said. He walked over and with no preliminaries, he picked Olivia up, placing her on his left shoulder as Sean did in the cheer. But he lifted her so abruptly, she nearly fell. She grabbed onto his shoulder for balance and he shoved her roughly back into place.

"Wait a minute! Couldn't you tell me what you're doing first?" Olivia really resented being hauled around like a sack of potatoes. For some reason, she had noticed, a lot of people treated small women as though they were completely insignificant.

"What's your problem?" Slammer shot back at her. He let her slide off his shoulder, and the two of them faced off, glaring at each other. "All right, I'll try it with your opposite number. You!" he called to Hope.

"Her name is Hope," Peter pointed out.

"And that's Olivia," Sean told Slammer between clenched teeth. "We have names, in case you're interested."

"Mr. Akins," Tara cut in. "We have a rule that you always tell somebody before you pick her up so she has a chance to get ready."

"And we usually talk the problem out before we try to make corrections on it," Jessica added. "But just what did you think was the matter with that cheer, anyway? If you don't mind my asking."

"Sam, can I talk to you a second, please?" Mrs. Engborg bit her lip and walked him over to one side of the gym so that the kids couldn't hear what they were saying.

"Oh, come on!" Sean said, grabbing Olivia's hand. "You have to object to this now, before Mrs. Engborg goes off to the hospital. We can't deal with this creep for two hours, let alone until Mrs. Engborg comes back."

Olivia nodded solemnly. "You're right. But I have a feeling this is a test. He wants to see how tough we are, if we can take it. And I think the best course of action is just to do our own thing."

"Uh-uh. No way is that going to work," Sean protested. "If the guy doesn't ease up, I'm walking. And I'm going to suggest that we all boycott practices here and get together on our own, in Tara's rec room or something."

Jessica shook her head. "They could disqualify us if we refuse to practice with the school's coach. Right, Olivia?"

"I just bet they will. Look," Olivia said, glancing over her shoulder at the two adults who were still engaged in a very heated conversation, "let's do it for Mrs. Engborg. She wouldn't have let him be put in charge if she thought it would jeopardize our chances. Remember how she said we've been too dependent on her, how we have to fend for ourselves now? Well, we can. We can practice his way and perform *our* way. And who knows? Maybe all this dumb running around and doing jumping jacks will tone up our muscles some more. C'mon, while they're still talking, let's show them our stuff. The 'Numbers' cheer."

Six determined cheerleaders assembled again and started their herky jumps in succession.

"And one and two,
We're here for you!
And three and four,
Let's mop up the floor!
And five and six,
Just watch our tricks!
Seven, eight, nine,
Stayin' right on line!
Tarenton, you're a ten!
Yay!"

The boys back-flipped to the center and ended in an arch, with Jessica and Olivia holding Tara's and Hope's legs up at their shoulders. They had big grins on their faces as they stopped and looked over to where the coaches had been.

But Mrs. Engborg was gone. Slammer Akins stood there alone, his arms folded across his chest and a fierce expression on his face. "All right," he began. "I want the handsprings crisp, right in sync. And the lifts, guys! You look like you're heaving ten-ton weights. It should seem easy. What about that back walkover you all do? Some of you have it, some of you don't. Let's try it from the top."

With heavy hearts and tired limbs, the cheerleaders went back to the beginning. It wasn't fun the next time, and it was just a job the time after that. And by the tenth time, it was bland and lifeless, purely mechanical.

They were depressed and exhausted when they quit at six o'clock. And the worst part was, they'd have to come back tomorrow and face Slammer Akins all over again.

"I just wish. . . ." Tara whispered as they walked slowly to the lockers.

"That he'd go away?" Jessica prompted.

"That it was *his* knee instead of Mrs. Engborg's?" Peter suggested.

"That he would suddenly turn into a math teacher?" Hope ventured.

"Or that he would take a running dive off a very short pier?" Sean said affirmatively.

"No," Tara continued. "I just wish the regionals were over. I don't even care if we win anymore."

Olivia wanted to tell her to cheer up, to put on a happy face, but it was useless. They would just have to plug along and work hard, and maybe, if the fates smiled down on them, Slammer Akins wouldn't make that much of a difference.

CHAPTER

The sign at the reception desk read: VISITORS FROM 3 TO 6. PLEASE TAKE A PASS. The clock on the wall told them it was 5:45. Sam Akins had kept them doing the same two routines over and over again, until *he* was blue in the face.

"I hate hospitals," Jessica murmured, remembering the awful sight of Patrick's face against the starched pillows when he'd been recovering from pneumonia. White on white, like all the blood had been drained out of him.

"This is nothing!" Sean joked. "Think how much worse it is going to one of these places if you aren't a visitor. Then they make you stay and eat the food!" He shuddered in mock horror.

"Hey, we've got the Tarenton High cafeteria," Tara reminded him.

"True," Peter chimed in. "But at least we can go out to Benny's after school. Mrs. Engborg's stuck here."

Olivia and Hope had signed in at the desk

and came back to the group, bearing six pink passes.

"The lady says we can only stay half an hour," Olivia told them. "The day after surgery, they like their patients to get lots of rest."

The kids took the elevator to the sixth floor and started down the corridor in search of Ardith's room.

"Excuse me. Just where do you think you're going?" A stocky nurse with a tight gray permanent stopped them right in front of their coach's door. She crossed her arms over her chest and glared at them.

"We're here to see Mrs. Engborg. We're from her school."

The nurse examined them with a critical eye, then looked at her watch. "It's nearly six, which means visiting hours are about over. Come back tomorrow."

Olivia had just about had it. "We won't be long," she said firmly. "And Mrs. Engborg wants to see us."

A welcome voice floated through the door. "Is that my team? Well, come in, for heaven's sake. What are you standing around out there for?"

Sean smiled broadly at the nurse. "If you'll just let us go in, I think somebody in there would like to see us."

The nurse's mouth made a straight line across her face. "Fifteen minutes. And that's all!" She stalked away as the cheerleaders hurried into Ardith's room.

The sight that greeted them was unsettling. Their coach was almost invisible in the mass of machinery and paraphernalia surrounding and encasing her. The bed was housed inside a metal frame, which had a big steel bar running across the top of it. The gigantic hoist worked on a series of metal weights, some of which were hooked up to the two poles that supported Mrs. Engborg's left leg. The unfortunate limb, bandaged to twice its size, was suspended in the air like a crane.

"Oh, no," moaned Hope.

"I guess you can't make a quick getaway, huh," Sean commented.

"You don't know how happy I am to see you." Mrs. Engborg grinned. "It's incredibly boring in here." She waved at the sterile green walls and TV set mounted high on the opposite wall.

"Why are you. . . ?" Jessica paused, trying to be tactful. "Why do they have you all hung up like that?" She had imagined her coach recovering with a small, neat ace bandage around her bad knee. And maybe a cane to get around with until the leg was strong enough. This contraption made it look like Ardith Engborg wouldn't — or couldn't — walk for months.

She shook her head, more in annoyance than worry. "I know it looks bad, but it's just the way they do things these days. High-tech medicine and all that. Doctors want you to feel you're getting your money's worth."

"When will you be out of here?" Olivia whispered, with desperation in her voice.

Mrs. Engborg shrugged. "Beats me. Probably no more than a few weeks. And then I may have to stay home for a few more." She paused. "How are things?" The look on her face told

74

them she was aware they might not be too happy with her replacement.

"Well, the 'Sharp' cheer is getting really fast," Olivia offered. She didn't think complaining about Slammer right off the bat would be such a great idea.

"And my stomach is incredibly flat from all those Royal Canadian Air Force push-ups with a clap in the middle that we do after warm-up," Peter added.

Mrs. Engborg raised one eyebrow. "Anybody else?"

"Mr. Akins has a van, so we can all ride to Lembrook together instead of going in two cars," Jessica mentioned, because that was the only positive thing she could think of. She was bursting to say what she really felt.

Tara said it for her. "None of us gets along with your substitute, Mrs. Engborg. He's simply horrible. He doesn't understand a thing about us or what we're like as people or how we function. And he doesn't care. I hate to bring this up, but. . . ." She tossed her red hair defiantly and sat down on an edge of the bed. Then, realizing that she might disturb the balance of the airborne leg, she popped up again. "But I have to."

"He's holding us back instead of pushing us ahead," Sean agreed, adding fuel to her fire. "It's like he doesn't even want us to place in the regionals."

Mrs. Engborg sighed deeply, then clasped the bar above her bed to pull herself up to a semi-sitting position. "I had a feeling that Slammer wasn't the best choice for this job. But Mrs. Oetjen insisted. And he is a wonderful athlete. He's done incredible things with all the Little Leaguers he's ever coached, not to mention the high school kids who've gone on to win full athletic scholarships to terrific colleges after being on his team."

"But that's the point." Olivia came over to stand beside the bed. "He treats us like we're a ball team. Like he can bully us into doing a good job. But we're artists — "

"Oh, come off it, Livvy. Let's not get carried away," Sean objected.

Hope giggled. "We may not be ballet dancers, Sean, but we are graceful . . . sometimes."

"Listen, we don't want to gripe," Peter said quietly, "but we are nervous about the big event. Tarenton did so well in competition last year, and it would be a real shame if we fell back in the ranks. We have so much going for us, Mrs. Engborg. Except our new coach doesn't see it that way."

Ardith Engborg rubbed her hands over her face. They were asking for her help, and she was completely powerless to do a thing for them. "I think you should talk to him," she said at last. "Be just as honest with him about your feelings as you have been with me. Don't hold back."

"And get our heads sliced off!" Sean looked at her in amazement. "The man doesn't treat us like equals, Mrs. Engborg. We'd probably get detention for objecting to his style of coaching."

"We'd all have to stay after practice and write 'I will not question authority figures' a hundred

76

times in chalk on the gym floor," Tara chimed in. "No, that's not the answer. That's only going to make him madder at us."

Everybody began talking at once, agreeing with Sean, complaining about Mr. Akins, and objecting vehemently to being treated so badly. The nurse came barreling through the door.

"What do you think this is?" she stormed, shooing them away from Mrs. Engborg's bed. "A zoo? You're making entirely too much noise, and visiting hours have been over for twenty minutes. Out. No back talk. I want you out."

"See," Sean said to the coach. "Even she won't let us get in a word edgewise. Another authority figure."

It was at this point that Mrs. Engborg put her foot down — figuratively. "That's enough. I know this is difficult for you, and I'm sorry about it, but now you're just whining. I wish you could hear yourselves. Once again, you're depending on me to make things better for you. Well, I simply can't. You'll have to take charge and make the situation better — without my help."

"Well. . . ." Olivia thought that, as group captain, she was in some way responsible for the rest of them. And yet she couldn't just act like everything would be nice and fine and they would all turn into good little girls and boys who would allow themselves to be pushed around. "I suppose there's a need for compromise in everything," she equivocated. "By everyone."

"Listen," Sean walked over to Mrs. Engborg and gave her shoulder a friendly pat. "You take care. We'll work it out."

"Yeah," Peter muttered.

"We'll come see you again soon," Hope promised as she started for the door behind the others.

Only Tara and Jessica remained in the room, standing on opposite sides of the bed. Both of them wanted some form of reassurance from the woman who had meant so much to them for so many months.

"You two will survive," Mrs. Engborg said, reading their faces. "You all will."

"I guess," Tara began, "that it's like a blind date. You don't know what you're getting into until you're right in the middle of it."

"Tell you what." Jessica shrugged. Her brow was deeply furrowed, as it always was when she was thinking hard. "I'll stop fighting him for a week. Just do everything he says without an attitude. And maybe that'll rub off on him."

"Fat chance," Tara scoffed.

"What about it, Tara?" Mrs. Engborg demanded. "Will you try, too?"

"Oh, all right." She threw up her hands. "I know when I'm beat." She shook her finger in Jessica's face. "But if you're wrong, and he's *still* obnoxious after five days of groveling, I'm going to turn right around the next week and give it to him with both barrels."

Jessica grinned happily. "And I'll load the weapons — how about that?"

Tara smiled and stretched out her hand across the bed and its mechanical contraption. Jessica grasped it firmly. "You've got a deal." Tara nodded.

"I don't envy that man," said Ardith Engborg.

The two girls left the room arm in arm, but when they reached the end of the corridor, Jessica suddenly turned to her friend, frowning. "Wait a second. I just thought of something."

Tara looked at her questioningly.

"If our plan doesn't work — I mean, if we end up going to war with him, what are we going to do about the regionals?"

Tara paused a minute, then shook her head. "I don't have an answer for that one. But I'm not going to let him pull us down. How about you?"

"Of course not." But as they walked down the hall toward their friends, they both had a sinking feeling. They wanted to prove Slammer wrong — but the consequences of being right could be really awful.

They told the other four about their plan right before practice the next day. Sean was skeptical; Peter was absolutely silent and expressionless; Olivia thought that it was worth a try; and even though Hope objected, on the grounds that they might end up doing themselves some injury, she said she would go along with the others for the week. After all, what was five days in the scheme of things?

After the first had passed, they were all convinced that five days would be longer than eternity.

"Get her up there faster!" Slammer yelled at Peter in the middle of their aerial work. "By the time you've got the girl on your shoulder, it's too late. Aren't you strong enough, or what?"

Peter swallowed hard. "You're right. I'll work on my arms. Couple of hours with weights over the next few weeks ought to help."

"Yeah, maybe," Slammer scoffed. "And Olivia, when you take off from his shoulders, I want you to ball yourself up real tight, like a snail under attack, okay?"

"That's a good idea." She smiled agreeably. "Thanks."

"Jessica, can you and Hope link hands sooner? If you catch her coming right off of Peter, right here, above her wrist, you'll get much better leverage."

"I see what you mean." Jessica nodded. "Now why didn't I think of that?"

They were trying too hard to be nice, falling all over themselves in an attempt to go along with every suggestion. And the net result was mass confusion.

The cheerleaders were used to instinctive timing that took a lot of experimentation with balance and gravity. The reason they were so perfect together was the give and take they always had. They subtly maximized on each other's strong points and covered for each other's limitations. The best of all of them shone through.

Slammer was insisting that they all do the moves identically. He made them repeat things over and over, aiming for speed and lock-step rhythms. And by the end of the afternoon, they had nearly undone all the good work it had taken them months to accomplish.

They were in the middle of a particularly complicated pyramid when the gym doors opened and Patrick and Pres walked in. The two made a habit of watching the end of the practice whenever their busy work schedule allowed it. They were always quiet, respectful of the cheerleaders' need for complete concentration. But they were helpful, too, because they provided the much needed audience for many of the group's new routines. And, of course, Jessica thrived on Patrick's loving looks — it made her feel all warm inside just knowing he was there.

The two guys took seats on a top bleacher as the work progressed. They could see that the team was in trouble. They could also see that they were not getting much positive feedback from the new coach.

"I don't like that spread eagle one bit, Olivia. Let's try pumping it up a little, okay? Like this — " As Slammer turned her around to show her something, he caught a glimpse of the two spectators. "And just who do you think *you* are?" he demanded, his hands on his hips.

Pres smiled winningly. "I think I'm Pres Tilford. And I'm pretty sure this is Patrick Henley. At least he was last time I looked."

Slammer began walking slowly toward the bleachers.

"This is going to be bad," Peter whispered to Tara. "See the way he's got his fist all jammed into his pocket?"

"What makes you think you can just waltz in here and interrupt a rehearsal?" Slammer asked pointedly.

"We're not interrupting, Mr. Akins," Patrick offered. "Mrs. Engborg always likes to have an audience for part of practice. It gives the kids kind of an extra edge, you know."

"I give these kids all the edge they need, thank you very much." Slammer marched right up to the bleachers. "All right, I have just one thing to say to you two. If I ever catch you in here again while I'm working, you'll be out so fast, you won't even know what hit you."

"Oh, yeah?" Pres asked, standing up. He loved a challenge.

"Hey, you've got no cause to talk to us like that," Patrick objected. "First off, we're not students here, and second, we were only — "

"Oh, you don't even go to this school?" Slammer yelled. "In that case, I might just call the cops."

"Pres, Patrick!" Olivia ran over, nearly tripping in an attempt to come between the two furious boys and the equally enraged Slammer Akins. "Please," Olivia said firmly. "Please leave now!"

Pres paused, then stepped down from the bleachers. His nose was inches from Slammer's. "We'll go. But because *you* asked us to, Livvy."

The cheerleaders were silent as Pres and Patrick made their way across the gym. And then, just as they knew he would, Slammer barked at them to get moving.

At six o'clock, when they were all on their last legs, the coach blew the whistle hanging around his neck. He was hot and angry, and he stormed around the gym like a mad bull. "For crying out loud, I thought I had some potential here, but all I can see are six losers. It's disgusting, you know. I mean, anybody watching you would think you'd never done this before. But that's okay with me. I'm used to grinding dumb kids into great athletes — no matter what it takes. If you're going to act like you don't know what the heck you're doing, I'm going to treat you that way. So starting tomorrow, I'm setting up a nutrition and exercise program for you."

The cheerleaders exchanged glances. Their silence could have been cut with a knife.

"I've found that the best treatment for lazy bodies is putting the right stuff inside them," Slammer continued. "Gets the muscle tone up, gets the mind in shape. That means no more Cokes, pizzas, or junk food. Strictly health food. You are what you eat."

"Excuse me, Slammer," Hope interjected, "but we really know all that. We may stray from the straight and narrow once in a while — "

"Yeah, like every day." Sean chuckled.

" — but we really know all about what an athlete's diet should be," Hope finished.

"No, you don't. It shows in your work. And that goes for smoking, too. Bad for the breath control. First one of you I catch with a pack of smokes is off the squad. Not to mention alcohol. I've seen kids ruined on smoke and drink, let me tell you."

"Oh, really," Olivia said with a small laugh. "None of us would smoke or drink. It's just plain dumb — we'd be hurting ourselves if we did. Anyhow, Mrs. Oetjen has strict rules about that."

"Rules are *always* broken by you teenagers.

I know you better than you know yourselves," Slammer sneered. "So tomorrow, we start a new system of working out. No more routines, no more cheers. Just exercise. And you'll follow my diet down to the last carrot stick. You know what the problem with you guys is? You've been mollycoddled and told that you're real hot stuff. You've got every Tom, Dick, and Harry walking in here whenever they want so you can show off for them. Well, let me clue you in, folks — those cute little routines you do are not exactly Olympics material. Maybe a few days in the trenches will convince you of that." He glared around the circle. "Okay, dismissed."

Jessica stood up unsteadily. She felt like a total hypocrite as she spoke words that she didn't mean. "We really appreciate what you're doing for us. It's bound to get results."

"Right." Slammer wiped the perspiration off the top of his head and marched quickly into his office.

Slowly and painfully, the six cheerleaders started for the showers. "Results," Sean muttered as they walked solemnly out of the gym. "I hate to think what'll happen to us if he gets what he wants. The nerve of that guy, telling us we're all a bunch of lazy, no-good, smoking, drinking fiends."

"It's like he doesn't have an ounce of respect for any of us." Tara sighed.

And the only thing the others could think of was that they had four more days ahead of them to agree to do everything he told them to.

CHAPTER

"I bet this is the stupidest movie ever made," Jessica said as she stood with Patrick outside the theater on Main Street and looked at the poster. It was a picture of a bloody hand with long black fingernails emerging from a mirror, about to strangle a completely unsuspecting heroine.

"It looks awful," Patrick admitted, "but we're the only two people left in town who haven't seen it. Hey, what's four bucks apiece, anyhow? Let's do it."

They stopped for popcorn, then started down the right aisle. The house lights were half-dimmed, so that you could see a few familiar faces in the crowd.

"This has to be the fifth time Ray and Tara have seen this movie." Patrick laughed.

"Well, he *is* kind of the gruesome type, wouldn't you say?" Jessica laughed. But the smile froze on her face when she spotted the couple seated a few rows behind her teammate and the basketball star. It was Mary Ellen and Pres.

"Let's go," she said, suddenly turning and starting back up the aisle.

"Hey!" Patrick barred her way. "You agreed to sit through this with me. Anyhow, it'll be kind of fun to grab each other during the scary parts."

"Look, we can do that anywhere. I'm serious — I don't want to stay." After the awful week she'd had, she just didn't want to run into Mary Ellen and have to stand around outside making small talk about how silly the movie was. And the theater was very small — it would be almost impossible for the two couples to miss one another on the way out.

"I don't see why you can't — " Patrick followed the direction of her gaze and suddenly understood. He sighed deeply. "That still bothering you?"

"Oh, Patrick, it's not that I think you're carrying a torch or anything. It's just . . . awkward. I'd prefer to avoid it."

"I promise, there'll be nothing to avoid. We'll see the movie, then leave during the credits. No sweat."

Jessica exhaled sharply, thought a second, and then reluctantly agreed. Patrick was probably right — she was just being paranoid. She sat down and begin to eat her popcorn, and then the movie started.

But all during the film, even the scary parts, she was preoccupied. She had hoped that the gore and screams and weird goings-on on-screen would help take her mind off her problems, but instead they just intensified them.

When the heroine in the movie walked into the school bathroom and started combing her hair in the very mirror that was going to be responsible for her demise later on, Jessica could only think of her own experience. She remembered standing in front of the mirror in the locker room after Friday's practice. She had done a triple flip on the minitramp, just the way Slammer had told her to, but she'd landed badly, tensing her neck at the last moment. She could still feel the crick in it.

When the heroine went out for a pizza with the hero, and the mozzarella and tomato sauce suddenly turned into a writhing mass of snakes, Jessica thought glumly of dinner the previous night with her mother and stepfather. Daniel was always after her about something or other. This time it was the letter from school he was supposed to sign, giving Jessica permission to go to Lembrook for the regionals. He reminded her that the day of the competition was his aunt Ruth's birthday party. He had specifically told her a month ago that he expected her to attend. And Jessica had persisted that she'd told him right back that it was out of the question because she had to go to Lembrook.

"Hey!" Patrick was whispering in her ear.

"Huh? What?" Jessica snapped out of her fog.

"This is the good part. You're not concentrating. The girl's about to fight the monster in the swimming pool."

"I'm sorry, Patrick." She smiled. The projector light flickering on his face made him look handsomer than ever, she thought. "This just isn't my kind of thing, I guess."

"Do you want to leave?"

A voice behind them boomed, "Will you two keep quiet!"

Jessica shook her head as if to say she didn't care. But she suddenly had an urge for more popcorn, so she took their empty container and walked to the back of the theater. She had just put her hand on the door when she felt someone behind her. And when she pushed it open and walked out into the lobby, her heart sank. Mary Ellen Kirkwood had obviously had the same idea.

"Oh, wow! Hi!" Mary Ellen laughed. "Not wild about the flick?"

"What?" In Tarenton, nobody called movies "flicks." "Um. Not really. And you?"

"Can't stand it. Pres insisted, so I said I'd go, as long as he'd take me out for a good dinner afterward." She threw up her hands. "But how am I ever going to extract him from that den of horrors?"

Jessica was trying to think of a clever answer when the door to the theater opened again and Pres and Patrick appeared.

"Well, look who's here!" Pres exclaimed.

"We're waiting out the gory parts. When the girl or the monster wins, we'll come back," Jessica told him.

"Aw, you two are no fun!" Pres complained lightly, taking Mary Ellen around the waist. "I can't believe you don't want to see how it turns out. I ran into Patrick on my way up the aisle to see what happened to you and Mary Ellen," he explained. "What about it, Melon? I don't suppose I can persuade you to go back in there?"

She made a face. "Not on your life."

"And you?" Patrick asked Jessica.

"Uh-uh," she responded firmly.

"Okay," Pres said. "I promised my date here I'd treat her to a meal, so we're off. Finally got my wheels back, thanks to that job in Laurence we did on Thursday. The baby runs like a dream. You two want to climb in back and join us?"

"Sure." Patrick nodded.

"Oh, we couldn't," Jessica said at the same time.

Patrick was immediately sorry he'd agreed, because Mary Ellen and Pres wouldn't take no for an answer. A very miserable Jessica finally smiled and said she'd changed her mind. She'd go.

Jessica climbed into Pres's car first, then Patrick wedged his large body in beside her. He ducked his head and scrunched down, but there still wasn't enough room in the tiny backseat for his long legs..

Pres and Mary Ellen got in and closed their doors.

"This is like one of those little cars at the circus," Patrick grumbled, "with too many clowns inside."

"Don't you say a word about this vehicle," Pres warned him. "Or you walk."

"That would be preferable," Patrick said emphatically, but they were already moving, so all he could do was try not to jam Jessica against the side. He kept her hand tightly clenched in his throughout the entire two-mile journey.

They stopped at Vesuvio's, a pizza place just on the outskirts of town. "Oh, Pres, you can't want pizza after that movie!" Mary Ellen protested.

"I do want it! I want four slices," he smiled. "C'mon. I promise, this place is fantastic. Besides, you guys will be permanently stuck in the back if you have to stay in there any longer. Everybody out!" he ordered. Then he stretched a hand out to his partner and gave Patrick's arm a yank. "Just for subjecting you to that painful experience, I'm paying, okay?"

"Oh, you don't have to do that," Jessica said quickly, remembering Pres's financial problems.

"No, really." He took Jessica's hand and started to lead her toward the front door. "I want to. You took care of me before — it's only right."

Jessica smiled. She was starting to like Pres a lot more.

Pres and Jessica made their way to the back, where there were a couple of available tables. Pres led her past the counter and waved a hello to the pie man, who was tossing a circle of floury dough up near the ceiling. "I could have done that," he said, grinning at Jessica, "if I hadn't decided to move furniture."

She laughed. "Somehow, I don't see you behind a pizza, Pres." Then she looked around anxiously. "Where's Patrick? Where are they?" she demanded.

"Somewhere between the anchovies and the mushrooms. Jessica, you can't do this to yourself," Pres told her solemnly.

"Do what?"

"You are so eaten with jealousy every time Mary Ellen comes into town — it sticks out all over you."

She looked at the floor. "Is that true? I was hoping it didn't show." She never liked to think of herself as somebody who wanted what didn't belong to her, or envied another person for her success. Except that in this case, she had to acknowledge, it was hard to look at Mary Ellen and smile. And *mean* it.

"Aren't you the least little bit worried? I mean, she and Patrick were so close," Jessica frowned.

"No, as a matter of fact, I'm not. I know what they used to be, but that's over." Pres leaned over to give Jessica a friendly bop on the nose. "There is only one thing that should concern you. . . ."

"What?" she demanded, nervous all over again.

"What you want on your pizza?"

Jessica didn't think she could laugh, but she did. She felt the burden of all she'd been through with the coach this week rolling off her. All the pressure, the competition, the offhanded remarks from her stepfather, the anxiety about this double date. First it was a giggle, bubbling from her throat, then a chuckle that moved inexorably down to become a huge belly laugh. The tears ran down her cheeks; she couldn't stop herself.

By the time Patrick and Mary Ellen arrived at the table, her mascara was smeared and her face was red, and even though she wished she could go to the ladies' room and get control of herself, there was just no way her jelly legs would carry her all the way across the restaurant.

"Well, you two certainly seem to be enjoying yourselves," Patrick smiled indulgently.

"I'm . . . I'm sorry." Jessica choked down one last guffaw, finally calming down.

"Don't be," Pres told her with a wink. "There should be more laughter in the world. And now" — he got to swipe the menus the waitress had left on the next table — "we should order."

"Good idea." Mary Ellen had a distinct feeling that she knew what Jessica's laughing fit was about, and that it had something to do with her. She knew that Jessica wasn't comfortable around her, and that made her kind of sad. She had had enough rejection in New York City.

They ordered, then Patrick said something about how hungry he was, and then there was an awkward silence at the table.

"Well, how's the new coach working out?" Mary Ellen asked, thinking it was a perfectly viable topic of conversation. But the looks on the faces of the other three told her she had made a big mistake. "Not so great, I guess," she said when no one spoke.

"He's a monster. You know, the fire-breathing,

earth-destroying variety," Pres ventured. "Other than that, I'd say he was a real good choice for the team."

"Pres!" Jessica shook her head at him hopelessly. "I don't really want to talk about it," she said cryptically.

"Oh?" Mary Ellen was suddenly curious, but she knew enough not to ask any more. Pres would tell her later.

The pizza arrived, and then they were too busy eating to make any small talk at all. But the mood had changed again, because suddenly there was an extra guest at the table. No one could see him or hear him, but he was a palpable presence. Not a friendly one, either.

"Hey," Pres said to Mary Ellen after they'd left the other couple back at Patrick's truck and were driving up Main Street, "let's make it a point not to do that again."

"Sorry. It was my fault."

"No. It was mine. I mean, I think Jessica is a great girl, and Patrick's like my alter-ego these days, but the combination of the four of us just doesn't wash. Know what I mean?"

"I'm sorry to hear the squad is having so many problems," Mary Ellen sighed. "It's weird — I've been away from it less than a year, and I still feel right in the middle of it. Being a cheerleader was so important, so much a part of our lives. In a way, it always will be."

"I feel the same way." He pulled into the driveway of her house and turned off the ignition, laughing softly to himself. "You know, I never could have told anybody else about it."

She looked at him intently, her blue eyes taking in the person she had known and the person he had become in such a short time. "What did you get out of cheering?"

"Everything." He shrugged. "It taught me discipline and teamwork. Much as I hate to admit it, something penetrated my thick skull last year. You know, it was rebellion at first — I joined the squad just to get back at my father. But I don't think I ever would have been able to go into business with Patrick and make a go of it if I hadn't learned what cooperation was all about."

She nodded. She had been there, too. Pounding the streets of New York would have been more than she could bear if it hadn't been for the groundwork she had as a determined cheerleader. "I got all that, and something else, too," she said after they had been silent for a minute or so. "I discovered what it was like being out in front, in the spotlight. I found out how good that felt. What I didn't know until recently was that performing just so the crowd would love me was doing it backward. If *I* don't feel good about myself, then having a lot of strangers clap and scream won't make a bit of difference."

Pres sighed and leaned his head back on the seat. "You're so grown-up," he said.

She laughed. "So are you. I never thought I'd be able to say that to you, of all people."

"Take it back!" he joked. "It isn't true. I only try to make it look that way." He was blushing hard, and thankful that the darkness covered up his embarrassment. "Listen," he went on, "I

94

wish you'd go share your great wisdom with those six kids. They're really down these days. I don't know how Mrs. Engborg could ever have agreed to let Slammer Akins take over. It's like letting a hit-and-run maniac drive a school bus. You ought to see this creep in action."

"Well, is he a good coach, at least?"

Pres shrugged. "He seems to know what goal he's aiming for — he just can't figure out how to get the team there without killing somebody."

"They've got to fight back," Mary Ellen said emphatically. "Let him know that they can't be pushed."

Pres put his arms around her. She was so lovely this way, her golden hair dusted with silvery moonlight. "If they're good enough, they'll come out on top despite him. They're very good, too."

She smiled. "You sound like you care a lot about them."

"I do. Kind of like an older brother, you know. Which is not, incidentally, the way I feel about you." He drew her to him, but before their lips met, they stared long and deep into one another's eyes. There was a new understanding between them, a sense of sharing born of this reunion. Only a year ago, they had dated just to be seen together, purposely never being serious when they could help it.

His mouth came down on hers, and her hands were in his thick, dark hair. She had an amazing and wonderful feeling. She had found a home — in Pres Tilford's arms.

CHAPTER

8

There were only five days to go before the regionals. The red and white uniforms were at the cleaners, the banners and posters had been finished, the schedule had been handed out. Tarenton High was sixth up to perform, right after St. Cloud Prep, which had one of the most exceptional cheerleading squads around.

"I think I'll die if we don't even place," Tara said as she walked down the corridor toward the gym with Sean, Olivia, and Hope.

"You won't die," Olivia told her flatly. "You may, however, be laughed out of Benny's the next time you walk in. That's all." She felt simply awful, like this whole thing had gotten out of her control. She had hoped, as captain, that she could make a difference, but it wasn't true. Slammer talked right over her suggestions and discounted her abilities as a leader.

"We've been so nice," Hope said. "I thought it might have been catching."

"Okay," a voice boomed down the corridor. "Are we ready to give it all we've got? Had the weekend to rest up, so we're gonna have a great practice today — I can feel it!" Slammer Akins rubbed his hands together and did his characteristic jog in place. He was, as usual, revved up and ready to go. But one thing they all noticed — he seemed brighter, cheerier, as if he actually expected good work from them. Previously, he'd walked into the gym ready to tear them apart. Today, he seemed willing to put them back together afterward.

"I think those exercises we worked on last week are really going to pay off," Hope ventured as they all walked through the door together.

"You bet," the coach said, slapping her on the back.

Sean mumbled something and walked to the side of the gym to sit down and put on his kneepads. He was still adjusting them when Jessica and Peter, both out of breath, rushed in a few seconds later.

"Hey, hey, you guys — look smart!" Slammer hated anyone being late. He had made a point of that on Friday when Tara came in half an hour after practice was in session, even though she had an excuse from her French teacher. He seemed to take tardiness as a personal affront.

"We're really sorry," Jessica began, "but we had to see Mrs. Oetjen about the speeches for assembly next week. Peter and I are both giving them and — "

"You know," Slammer said to her, "I'm not interested in any other activities you kids are into. I expect full and complete attention to this squad. If I were really running this team, I'd make it a rule that my cheerleaders would have no other extracurriculars."

"Well, you're not," Sean pointed out.

"What was that?" Slammer was suddenly on guard.

"You're not running it. You're just the substitute."

Olivia could feel a fight coming on, and she quickly jumped in. "Well, we really ought to get to those cheers, since we didn't work on them at all last week. Why don't we start with the 'Pride' cheer and go onto 'Sharp'?"

The others agreed and before Slammer could say anything, they were in formation, ready to do cartwheels out from the center of the floor.

> "We're loud,
> Hear us yell!
> We're proud,
> Can't you tell?
>
> Standing tall,
> Got it all!
> T-A-R-E-N-T-O-N!
>
> Proud of our team,
> Here's what we mean —
> Tarenton Wolves, YAY!"

Hope, sitting on Peter's shoulders, and Olivia, on Sean's, had their arms raised high as the boys dropped to their knees and slid forward several yards while Jessica and Tara stood behind them, holding their outside legs high in the air. They posed in position for the end until Slammer walked over, scratching his head.

"You boys planning to wear those kneepads in the competition?"

"No, of course not," Peter said.

"Then why do you have them on now?"

"Mrs. Engborg's rule," Sean explained. "We take precautions during practice, all the way up to dress rehearsal."

"Well, what kind of sense does that make?" Slammer demanded. "Whatsa matter? Afraid to take a few falls? Get 'em off, both of you — right now. And move those crash mats. You don't need them, either. Girls, we need more oomph in that last set of flips."

"Okay," Hope agreed willingly. "Should we try it again?"

"You know, kids," Slammer began thoughtfully, walking around in a circle, "I've been with you a week now, and I just have this gut feeling that there's something missing. I mean, we can practice these moves till the cows come home, but we still won't have that special something that brands us as winners. So today, we're going to try a new scheme."

"Sure, coach," Jessica put in, remembering that she had to agree. But she had an uneasy sense that she was not going to like whatever it was that he wanted them to attempt.

"Okay, this is a competition. Two teams. You guys — Hope, Tara, Sean — over here. The other bunch, stay where you are. We're going to have a meet and compete for points. Whoever does the best forward rolls, flip-flops, back walk-overs, jumps, et cetera, wins."

"But we're a team *together*," Olivia objected. "That's the point of all this." She totally forgot that she wasn't supposed to question him.

"Sister, that looks real nice on paper," Slammer smiled at her indulgently. "But when you're out there, clawing your way to the top, you'll wish you'd had a little more of the animal in you. I want *real* team spirit — and what I mean by that is the kind of push that will send the other guy reeling. You've got to bite down and grab what you want out of life. Starting here."

He got them into two little huddles, as though they were football teams squaring off. Then he went over and whispered a few words of encouragement to each of them.

"First! On the minitramp, a double and a forward roll. C'mon, Olivia! I'm grading you on a one-to-ten basis for accuracy, grace, and spirit."

Olivia tentatively walked to the center and climbed onto the mini-tramp, springing up and down a little to start some momentum.

"Well, teammates!" Slammer challenged. "What are you waiting for? Give her support!"

Peter and Jessica gave Olivia a feeble rah-rah cheer, but their hearts weren't in it. The whole thing was completely ridiculous.

Olivia bounded into the air, then pulled her body in tight, whirling in space. She spun twice, landed, and sprang to the ground, tucking her head for the roll. Peter and Jessica were applauding loudly now, and so were Sean, Tara, and Hope.

"No! Hey, that's your enemy," the coach reminded the other team. "You want her to fail."

"I don't," Hope said staunchly. "I want her to do just as well as she did that time — all the time." Hope stood up and walked over to Olivia. "You were wonderful. As always." The two girls smiled and spontaneously embraced.

"Aw, what kind of tea party *is* this?!" Slammer was furious. "Didn't anything I said about group spirit penetrate? Olivia, your score was nine-nine-three. The three's for that sour look on your face. All right, Hope. You next. Try to do better."

Hope was livid. She performed the motions mechanically, like a perfect wind-up toy. She ended on the ground, in the correct position, with not a trace of enthusiasm.

Slammer didn't even look at her. Instead, he walked over to her teammates and took them both by a shoulder. "Are you going to let her get away with that, kids? Listen, you have exactly five days to go. Five — count 'em! You know what that means? At schools all over this region, your opposition is getting ready to slaughter you. And you six just sit back and take it! All right, Hope, that was a seven-six-two score. Pretty poor, wouldn't you say?"

"I suppose so," she agreed between gritted teeth.

"Can't you do anything right?" he prodded.

"I used to think I could," she answered angrily. She had never felt so impelled to lash out at somebody in her life, and yet she knew that the coach was doing this on purpose to get her riled. She would not give into his awful, aggressive tactics.

Peter, however, didn't seem to understand that this was a ploy. He got up and walked toward the coach, his tall, thin body a menacing coil of steel, about to spring. "You know, we've had about all we can take," Peter began.

The coach turned on him. "You mad?"

"Sure I'm mad! First you run us ragged for a week so we're too tired to even practice properly, and then you start on us today with this killer competition stuff. I don't think you have any idea what you're doing."

"So show me how to do it better." Slammer stood in front of him, grinning. It was a dare.

"Back off, Peter," Sean warned him.

"Oh, this is really dumb!" Jessica exploded. "Why don't we just go back to the cheers we have to perform, folks?"

"I think that's an excellent idea," Olivia stated, getting up and taking a position between Peter and the coach.

"No, I'm not finished," Peter growled, shoving her aside. "For a whole week, we decided we were going to go along with your method, do whatever you said. I don't suppose you noticed, but we were really trying to please you. Now I think it's about time you did things our way," he went on angrily.

"You do? You think that being part of this cheerleading team gives you the right to call yourself boss?" Slammer smiled at him meanly. "What kind of guy goes out for cheering, anyway? Answer me that?"

There was a hush in the room, as though an evil wind had just blown through it. Then Tara took a breath and went over to the corner to get her practice bag. "We're all too upset to accomplish anything today," she said. "C'mon, gang. Let's leave and meet over at my house."

"Oh, now you're running out on me, are you?" Slammer said, turning on her. "Can't take a little heat."

"I can take a lot of heat. We all can." Tara ran a hand through her fiery hair, feeling the impulse to show him running from her fingertips to her toes. "Just watch us." And then she gathered the other five around her and said just one word — "Sharp."

"All right," Peter agreed.

> "Make it sharp!
> Make it quick!
> Dynamite!
> Do it right!
> Make it stick!"

Hope and Olivia were like bullets, ricocheting around the boys' heads. From thigh stands, they moved to flying fishes, and then finally to triumphant shoulder stands. Jessica and Tara had never done their spread eagles so cleanly, nor had they ever slid down into such flat splits.

> "Like a shot,
> From a gun!
> Speed! Power!
> Now we've won!"

Hope didn't remember the sequence of events, but she must have lost her footing when she heard the coach's angry voice. She was just about to take Peter's hand so that she could get down from the shoulder stand, when Slammer yelled, "Hope! Not that way!" and she fell. One moment, she was high above her teammates; the next, she was lying on her side with her right arm pinned beneath her.

"Owww!" She was usually stoic, but this really hurt. The others gathered around her, and Peter knelt by her side.

"Are you okay?"

"I guess."

"You didn't sprain it, did you?" Olivia asked. She was staring at Slammer, furious but unable to speak. He had clearly caused this accident, and would never own up to it.

"No, I don't think . . . it just hurts a lot. It'll be okay," Hope murmured, testing the fingers.

"I'll take care of this," Slammer said, moving the others aside. "C'mon. It's not that bad. Just a little spill."

"A little spill that didn't have to happen," Tara was incensed. "The only reason she lost her balance was that your screaming distracted her."

"I can't believe I've got such a bunch of babies here." The coach knelt beside Hope and checked her carefully. He moved her arm slowly back and forth, asking her where the pain was. Then he tried the wrist and finally the hand and fingers.

"Well, looks okay to me. Guess you'll live," he joked.

"I'm really *fine*, now," Hope said, gritting her

teeth. She pulled her arm from his grasp, wrenching it painfully.

"I guess you don't want to try it again, do you?" he challenged. "Although the best medicine is to get right back on the horse, you know."

"Yes," Hope agreed, "but I think I should go home and soak the arm. If that's okay with you," she added.

"Hey, sure, if it'll make you feel better." Slammer shrugged. "You get somebody to drive you home and rest up. Get ready to work out tomorrow." He chuckled as he eased her up to a sitting position. "Everybody's a little klutzy once in a while. Happens to the best of 'em."

Nobody honored his statement with so much as an angry look. To see that Hope really hadn't been that badly hurt made them all so grateful, they figured it wasn't even worth trying to explain to this insensitive coach exactly why such a terrific cheerleader had fallen.

"Call me if it's not better by tonight," Jessica said softly. "I have this great liniment that might work."

Peter took Hope's hands as she nodded, and helped her, steadying her small form against his.

Hope straightened up and smiled. "I'll go get my gear out of the locker room."

"I'll take you home, and stay with you for a couple of hours," he told her.

The others were too busy looking after her to realize that Slammer had walked away and gone back to his office, closing the door behind him.

"If she can't perform on Saturday, I'll sue that man," Tara said defiantly. Then she turned around. "Oh, so he sneaked off!" She narrowed her eyes in the direction of the crash mats. "If we'd been working on the mats the way Mrs. Engborg always has us do in practice sessions, this never would have happened."

"Let's not waste precious time going over it all," Jessica said with fierce determination. "I'm going in there right now to straighten him out. I don't expect to wring any apologies out of him. I just want him to know that if he's ever going to coach another cheerleading squad, he can't treat it the way he's treated us. Someone could have been seriously injured." She stormed out of the gym, not waiting for the others to second her opinion.

"Just a second!" Olivia called, putting on speed to catch up with Jessica. "I want to know what you're going to say."

"Wait for me!" Peter insisted. "I have something at stake here."

"Oh, let me at him, please!" Tara begged, jostling Sean in her effort to get ahead of him. "I really could demolish that idiot."

"I hate to sound like my father, but this is a man's job," Sean stated.

The girls all stared at him in disbelief.

The five of them were at his door now, and Jessica put up her hand to knock.

"Just a minute," Olivia said, pulling her back.

"We can't all go in," Peter objected. "We'll end up yelling at him — it'll be a free-for-all."

"I agree," Tara nodded. "It should be one person. And I nominate me."

"No, me," Sean insisted.

Olivia could have laughed, had the circumstances been different. All of them wanted to get back at Slammer Akins. But more than that, they wanted to preserve the team.

"Listen," she suggested. "I'm captain, so let me decide. I think Sean and Peter should stay out of this. For some reason, Slammer gets that whole macho thing going when a guy challenges him on anything. I'm not saying the three of us should bat our eyelashes by any means — "

"I should say not!" Jessica cut in.

" — but we should stay cool. Remember, Mrs. Engborg expects us to take care of ourselves. Now, the only way we're going to do that is to act like adults and slowly but surely convince the man that he's been wrong and we only have four days to get it right — which means working *our* way for a change. Are you with me?"

Sean started to argue, but Tara overrode his objections. "You and Slammer haven't said a civil word to each other since Mrs. Engborg left. It would do more harm than good if you came in. Peter, you go take Hope home and let the three of us handle this. I promise we won't let you down," she concluded.

The two boys looked at each other, then at their teammates. "Okay," Peter agreed. "But give it to him, will you?"

Jessica smiled. "We will."

And then she took a deep breath, lifted her hand, and knocked.

"Come in," said Slammer Akins. "I've been expecting you."

CHAPTER

Jessica walked in first, flanked by Olivia and Tara. They approached cautiously, watching Slammer for any reaction. He was seated in a big chair that dwarfed the room, his feet up on the desk, holding a glass of some strange greenish-orange liquid. In front of him were an assortment of bottles of vitamins and juices. The mixed carrot-and-celery concoction, Olivia noticed, was the one he had just polished off. He looked comfortable, in his element.

"Well . . ." Jessica began.

"Girls, please, have a seat." He motioned to the only available place on the floor of the small office that wasn't jammed with files, papers, or books.

"No, thanks. We'll stand," Olivia told him. She remembered something she'd read about how it was always easier to negotiate if you were above your opponent. You put the other person on edge just by being taller.

"Okay, suits me. Hey, it's real nice that you came in for a chat, you know? Other teachers always seem to have kids hanging around after hours, but a gym teacher? That's the whole trouble with this department — we don't foster a spirit of getting things off our chest. And we should."

"I'm glad you brought that up," Olivia told him, "because we have a lot to discuss." She looked at the other two, asking for permission to go ahead and let him have it.

"But before you do," Slammer interrupted, "let me just say that I've been at a lot of schools, working with a lot of different kinds of teams, and Tarenton just takes the cake. You guys are something."

"Yes, well, we know you're not that impressed with the kind of approach we take to cheerleading," Tara said, "but we think — "

"Your approach is really interesting, really. Don't get me wrong. But what good is an approach without results?" Slammer demanded, getting up and walking to the window.

"What do you mean when you say we're really something?" Jessica asked suspiciously.

"Well, hey, I heard you had a reputation," he shrugged. "I heard you were the finest group of six athletes that had come down the pike in a long time, bar none. I must say, today at practice, before Hope fell, I had some hope for you — no pun intended." He chuckled. "But I'm disappointed. Seriously disappointed. I'd seen you at games even before Mrs. Oetjen asked me to come on board, so I had my work cut out for me. But

109

this is ridiculous. Any squad in the state could beat you."

The three girls just stared at him. *"What?"* Tara and Jessica said in unison. Tara sat down on the floor in total shock.

"You're no good. You're sloppy, badly coordinated, you project your cheers like a bunch of scared nursery-school kids." He folded his arms across his chest and stared at them coldly.

"I can't *believe* you think we're that bad," Olivia said.

"If you think we're so totally hopeless," Jessica interjected, "then why even bother with us?"

"A challenge," he told her. "Nothing I like better than hard work. Shows what mettle a *real* coach has when he can take the dregs, the pits, and turn them into a halfway decent team."

"Nobody else seems to think we're that terrible," Tara commented.

"There! That's your whole problem," Slammer exclaimed. "Everybody, Ardith Engborg and Mrs. Oetjen included, have led you to believe you're fantastic. They've filled your heads full of stories about how super you look on the court. That kind of treatment is going to be your downfall," he said in a voice of doom. "Well, I'm not afraid to tell you kids that you just haven't got it."

"Oh, really?" Olivia was past anger now. The three of them had come in here full of good intentions, wanting to help this man to look at things their way. Now, all she wanted to do was punch him in the nose. How dare he insult them like this!

Slammer walked over to them, his hands on his hips. "Never tell a ball player he's good — that's my motto. He gets weak, gets soft, sits back on his laurels. You have to keep 'em hopping, girls."

Olivia cleared her throat. "Well, we're not playing a team sport. Cheering is different. You can't pit one of us against another and expect us to do well. What we do . . . well, it's creative, it's changeable, it's different every time we do it. And the reason for that is because we're partners every step of the way."

He frowned, as though she'd spoken to him in a foreign language.

"Don't you see?" Tara said simply. "We need encouragement. We can't go on without it."

"Now, that's just too bad, isn't it?" he scoffed, throwing up his hands. "If you can't take a little criticism from me, how're you gonna stand up to those judges at Lembrook? Answer me that."

"We need to be able to work together," Jessica said slowly. "When you yell at us like you did today, it breaks our concentration. It tears us apart. Look what happened to Hope."

He shook his head. "Hope's okay. She's just a little sensitive. You're all too sensitive."

"Well, pardon us!" Tara said sarcastically.

He laughed, but it sounded more like he was laughing at her than with her. "Listen, kids. Don't try so hard to be creative. I'm going to get better work out of you with sweat and tears. That's my way."

Olivia shook her head. "No," she said bluntly. "That won't help us. We've tried it your way and

111

we're miserable. We've done our routines inside out and backward for you. We've done them double time and triple time — and what we've gained in speed, we've lost in excellence."

"I don't agree." He frowned. "You're just taking a little longer than most to get my method."

"But we know what you're doing isn't working for us. We can feel it!" Tara insisted. "A gymnast knows when the catches aren't right, or when the balance is off. And that's the state we're in right now. All the moves that used to flow between the six of us are chopped up. They're awful!"

"Please," Jessica was practically begging him. "We only have a few days left. If you don't give a little with us, all we'll have is stamina and endurance by the time we get to the regionals. You're breaking our spirit — can't you see that?"

But nothing had penetrated. "You know what your real problem is?" he asked the three of them. "You worry too much. From now on, let me do the worrying, how's that? We've got a long way to go in a few days, I'll grant you that. But I'm not against you — I'm for you. If you can get that fact through your heads by Saturday, you might just have a chance of placing. Even though I doubt it."

"We're sorry you feel like we've caused you so much trouble," Olivia said quietly. She could hear the sighs of her two teammates as she walked to the door, now resigned to this man's incredible lack of compassion and awareness. The day they were giving out hearts, she decided, Slammer Akins had been absent.

"Hey, no problem. I'm used to dealing with kids."

"Okay, well." Tara was fumbling around for a brilliant closing line, but there didn't seem to be any. "We thought it would be a good idea to go through all the routines in sequence before dress rehearsal Friday. Would it be okay with you if we did that tomorrow?"

"We haven't really gone over the standard cheers in a while," Jessica pointed out.

"I'll think about it," the coach said stolidly, not giving an inch. "If you're not as bad as you were today, we'll try it. Now I've got to get out of here, okay?"

Olivia hesitated a minute, wanting to say more, but she bit back the words, realizing it was futile. She turned without a word.

She felt his hand on her shoulder. "I'm real glad you felt we could talk and get all this out in the open," he said sincerely. "I hope this will be the first of many good bull sessions."

Tara closed the door behind them and started down the hallway, shaking her head. "The man's out of his mind," she muttered. "You say one thing, he hears another."

Jessica, walking beside her, was chuckling. "Maybe he's hard of hearing."

"That's possible," Tara giggled. "He yells so much it could have affected his eardrums."

Olivia was quiet, thinking it all through. It was puzzling, upsetting. They weren't bad — she knew that. At least they hadn't been until he started coaching them. And that was the terrible part. No matter what they did or said, Slammer

113

Akins was going to persist that his way was the only way. And their cheerleading squad could never win like that.

"Oh, no!" Jessica put a hand to her forehead. "In the midst of all that I left my book bag in there." She whirled around and started down the hall again. "Don't bother waiting. Patrick is picking me up."

She ran back and knocked hastily, not really wanting to go back in. But she had no choice. She had about four hours of homework ahead of her, and it was all sitting on the floor of Slammer Akins' office.

"Yes?" she heard him say as she pushed open the door.

"I left my — " Her voice trailed off as an acrid odor assailed her nostrils. The unmistakable smell of cigarette smoke. Slammer quickly walked over to his desk and stubbed out the offending butt in the cap of his empty juice bottle.

She was dumbfounded, almost too surprised to be angry. Was this the man who had lectured them about becoming perfect athletes, who was going to put them on strict diets, telling them that any deviation from his course would result in their bodies falling apart? Was he the person who had insisted that anyone who smoked or drank would be thrown off the squad? How could he sit there in front of them, guzzling some disgustingly healthy juice and pretending to be a paragon of self-discipline, and then, after all that, go and light up?

Slammer made no comment about the cigarette. He opened the window to let the smell out, and the winter afternoon came rushing in. Jessica shivered a little as she retrieved her book bag. Then she turned to him.

"Well, what are you staring at?" he asked.

"I thought you said that athletes shouldn't smoke."

"I did. And I meant it."

"Well, then, what's *that*?" She pointed to the butt.

"Listen to me, young lady. If it's any of your business — and it's not — I live clean," he said, gesturing toward the vitamins and juices.

"I see."

"I only have one of these a day. Helps me wind down."

"If it's bad for us, then why is it okay for you?" Jessica persisted.

"You're kids. I'm an adult. You think you could stop at one a day? Teenagers have to be led around on a very short chain."

"Uh-huh." Jessica couldn't help but think about Mrs. Oetjen's strict rule. There was no smoking anywhere on the school premises. Even the faculty lounge was off limits. And yet, here was this man, lighting up in his office. "I just came to get my books," she said, turning to leave.

"Jessica — " There was a warning note in his voice.

"Yes?"

He looked at her keenly, as if trying to decide whether she was a snitch. "If you so much as breathe a word of this, you're not competing on Saturday. They'll go on without you. Bad as it'll

115

be, it'll be worse — with one traitor thrown off the squad."

"Oh, you don't have to worry about me," Jessica said, her head held high. "I don't think it's even worth mentioning." Even though it would have felt great to dish some dirt about Slammer's smoking, it wouldn't help the team at all. Mrs. Oetjen was Slammer's friend, and it was doubtful that she'd even believe Jessica. She'd just think it was a feeble attempt on the part of a disgruntled student to make trouble.

"I'll keep my mouth shut," she continued. "But if you don't mind my saying so, you should, too. Every time you put another one of those terrible things between your lips, you're only harming yourself."

"Look who's giving lectures! You just concentrate on your routines, okay?"

She tossed her book bag over her shoulder and left the office, closing the door behind her.

It wasn't until she was halfway down the stairs on her way to the parking lot that she realized how perfectly all the pieces fit. A phys. ed. teacher who believed in downgrading his athletes, a vitamin nut who smoked cigarettes, a rah-rah enthusiast who thought that "slaughtering" the other guy was more important than having concern for your fellow team members. Slammer Akins was a beautiful example of a hypocrite.

A new discomfort crept over her. If she couldn't trust a thing he said, then how could she have faith in his statement that he was going to whip them into shape so that they could win? Maybe he wanted them to lose.

116

CHAPTER

Her feet flew down the stairs, out the front door into the parking lot. Tara and Olivia were standing beside Sean's car, talking animatedly. Well, wait till they heard Jessica's new piece of news! They'd fall over when she let that out.

And then it occurred to her that she couldn't tell her teammates about Slammer's smoking. If she'd promised him not to divulge his secret to anyone, then that included the cheerleaders. She grimaced, drawing her wool beret down around her ears. It was disappointing, but it didn't matter. There was enough to keep her busy on the subject of Slammer Akins.

She walked slowly toward the girls, but the sight of approaching headlights made her turn. She always knew Patrick's truck: The lights were at a higher level than all the other cars around. And soon she could see the painted red logo on the side, announcing his arrival.

117

She started running toward the truck as soon as it made the circle into the Tarenton High parking lot. But she stopped, one foot in midair, when she saw who was sitting in the passenger seat.

Mary Ellen looked positively ethereal tonight, her golden hair loose, swaying around her perfect head like sheaves of wheat in a field. She was smiling at the driver — Jessica could see her teeth gleam when she tossed her head. And then she put up one hand and gently touched his cheek.

Well, perfect! This was just great. She should have known better than to expect that Mary Ellen wouldn't eventually try to see if any of her magic still worked on Patrick. It was understandable, really. When you'd gone together with somebody as long as Mary Ellen had gone with Patrick, there had to be some tiny curiosity.

She was furious. How dare he even consider seeing that rotten, beautiful girl again? How could he drive around town with her, just like in the old days, knowing that absolutely everyone in Tarenton would see them — and then go off to gossip about how he was still stuck on Mary Ellen Kirkwood and Jessica was old news.

She stalked away toward the other end of the parking lot. She didn't want to go near Tara and Olivia now, and she had no intention of letting them — or anyone — see the tears in her eyes. They were angry tears, burning and shaming her.

Jessica rarely felt sorry for herself. She had succumbed to such feelings only twice before: when her father died and when her mother remarried. And each time, she had pulled herself out of her doldrums and gone right on. Now, standing in the cold, with the wind blowing right through her parka, she couldn't even imagine regrouping her emotional forces. She was ready to cave in.

So she didn't see Pres run out the front door of Tarenton High and go to greet Mary Ellen at Patrick's truck. She didn't see him whirl her down from the passenger seat and spin her around joyously. She didn't hear Mary Ellen's laughter, or see the delighted look on her face when Pres marched her away to his own waiting car. The next thing she was aware of was a pair of large hands covering her eyes.

"Who is it? Three guesses, and make 'em fast, will you? It's cold out here," Patrick teased.

Jessica yanked at his fingers, the anguish rising in her. She couldn't stand to have him anywhere near her.

"Ow. Hey, take it easy. You must have had it out with old Slammer today. Am I right?" he asked with concern in his voice.

She whirled around to face him. "What do you care if I did?"

He looked at her, puzzled. "Boy, that had to be some fight. Don't take it out on me, sweetie. C'mon, let's get in the truck and get over to your house."

"I already have a ride," she lied. "Thank you anyway." It was possible that Sean was still around.

"Jessica? You want to talk about something with me?"

She shook her head.

"Okay. All right." He threw up his hands.

"What did I do? What did I say? What didn't I say?" He rubbed one hand inside the other, piecing together all possible elements. "Oh . . . oh, I get it. You saw me and Mary Ellen drive in here just now. Jessica! How many times do I have to tell you — "

"None. Just, simply *none*. You can talk until you're blue in the face. So don't bother."

Suddenly, he was the one who was annoyed. "You are so insecure — do you realize that? I give an old friend a ride, and you make a federal case out of it. Well, I think that's a pretty sad statement about you and me."

"Mary Ellen Kirkwood is not, nor will she ever be, an old friend of yours, Patrick." Jessica was calmer now, as if she were outside the scene, watching it happen to someone else. "Anyone with eyes can see that. She was . . . she was patting your face, for heaven's sake!" she exploded.

"Jessica, she was telling me this story about putting on makeup for a modeling job. She was showing me how she did it." He sighed deeply. "You're never going to believe that I care about you."

"That's not the point! Don't you see? What we had together — what I thought we had," she corrected herself, "was caring based on honesty and openness. I thought we had the kind of relationship that counted, to the exclusion of everybody else."

"Oh, I see," he countered. "You want me to go live in a shell and hibernate — never even say hi to another girl. Well, I'm not that kind of person, Jessica."

"I didn't say that! I just meant — "

"I know what you meant. All right, be that way! Maybe I am still crazy about Mary Ellen and I just haven't been honest enough to admit it to you. Now are you satisfied?"

She stared at him in horror. It wasn't true — he had only said it to hurt her. Well, he had succeeded beyond his wildest imagination. She turned from him and ran, hoping that someone she knew would still be in the parking lot. When she spotted Sean's car, just pulling out of its space, it was like an oasis in the desert.

"Wait! Wait up!" she called, putting on more speed. She caught up with him at the stop sign at the entrance gate. "Sean, can you give me a lift?"

"Hey, yeah. The more the merrier. Climb aboard."

Tara and Olivia didn't ask one question as she collapsed in the backseat. They had both seen Patrick stalking away from his truck. And they had both known bad times themselves, times when you couldn't even talk about what you were going through because the words were simply too painful.

It was quiet in the car — uncomfortably so. Jessica could hear her own breathing. She knew the others didn't dare speak, because of the mood she was in.

This was ridiculous, she thought. She was behaving like a child. And she wasn't helping anyone, least of all herself. She certainly wasn't helping the team. As they turned the corner onto the street where Hope lived, Jessica bit the bullet." "Look," she said. "I have an idea. If Hope is okay, let's make a date for tomorrow night. And the next two nights, too. We're going to get our team back together again. And I know the way to do it."

"What have you got in mind?" Sean asked. "Kidnapping Mrs. Engborg from the hospital?"

"No. Getting good feedback. We haven't had anybody we really trust giving us criticism. But there are two people who could help — they both saw us at the game, at the peak of our form, just a couple of weeks ago. Pres and Mary Ellen." The name felt strange in her mouth, like a collection of tiny stones.

"You mean, we could ask them to come look at our work," Tara said.

"Sure," Olivia broke in, a smile flashing across her face. "They were cheerleaders, too. They understand what it takes to be number one. And most important, they know us and care about us. That's a terrific idea, Jessica!"

Jessica nodded and settled back in her seat as Sean parked in the Changs' driveway. Nobody would ever know what it cost her to take advice from Mary Ellen Kirkwood. She would be attentive, and listen, and if she was able to put on the greatest performance of her life, she might even smile.

The practice the following afternoon was a complete disaster, and the mistakes were the least of their worries. The coach was in a foul mood because nobody was paying attention to a thing he said, and not even Olivia could muster support for trying just a little harder. Peter actually forgot one of the cheers right in the middle of it — Peter Rayman, of the photographic memory! When the six teammates walked back to the lockers, sweaty and disgusted, none of them had much faith in their own abilities.

They met in Tara's rec room at seven sharp that night. She had cleared all the furniture to one side, and placed crash mats over the hardwood floor. The kids were ready, warming up, when the distinct sound of a Porsche's engine zoomed up close by, then quickly died out.

"They're here!" Hope said cheerily, looking out the window.

"You're sure you feel up to it?" Peter asked her.

"Don't mother-hen me," she warned him, feigning a friendly punch to his chin. "I'm looking forward to this."

"I'm sure we'll get something out of it," Jessica said, her stomach clenching as Tara's mother answered the door upstairs.

"Yeah, another two cooks putting in their oar," Sean grumbled.

"That's 'spoiling the soup,' isn't it?" Tara grinned.

"Whatever." Sean moved closer to her, while the others continued to talk about routines and moves. "You know, I didn't mention it earlier, but you look fantastic tonight. I don't think I've ever seen a lavender leotard before. At least, not on a luscious redhead." He gave her that winning smile that never failed to make her drop everything. "When all this is over, how about we go grab a Coke somewhere?"

Tara gave the invitation two seconds' thought. On the one hand, she was sort of bored with Ray Elliott. He was great-looking and tall and a basketball hero, but having a conversation with him was like dragging around a ten-ton weight. And Sean, despite his flirting and his attitudes, was a lot of fun. On the other hand, she wanted to keep him hanging, make him more interested than he was. "Gee, I'm sorry, Sean. I kind of have other plans. Ray said he'd drop by. Maybe sometime soon, though."

The door to the basement opened and Mary Ellen walked in, her cheeks pink, her eyes shining. Her right hand gave a tug, bringing Pres into view at the top of the stairs.

"Hi, guys. The judges are here," he sang out.

"What are we waiting for?" Mary Ellen asked. "Turn on the music and let's go!" She walked gracefully down the stairs, a model all the way, and pulled off her coat to reveal tapered jeans and a creamy wool sweater with a boat neck. She went over and took Olivia's clipboard from her, looking at the lineup of cheers.

Jessica's gaze could have cut a hole in granite. She was looking through everyone to the third figure standing at the top of the staircase, looming large in the doorway. Why in heaven's name had Patrick come?

"Okay," Olivia said, getting right down to business. "We're doing four routines at Lembrook. One is the standard formation cheer that every group has to do. You remember, Melon. We could do it in our sleep."

"That may be part of your problem," Mary Ellen laughed.

"You said it! Then we have the 'Pride' cheer and the long, jazzy thing that Holly Hudson choreographed for us. Those are both pretty shaky. The final piece, 'Sharp,' well, I don't know. It's a mess."

"We'll see." Mary Ellen sat down beside Pres against one wall and looked seriously at the group. "Listen, all of you. Pres and I are really thrilled that you asked us to come and watch. We'll do anything we can to counteract the ill effects of Slammer Akins, okay?"

"Well," Tara sighed, "that's a tall order to fill."

"We won't let you down," Pres promised. "Go ahead."

Jessica went over to turn on the tape recorder, and Olivia took them through their paces. They did all the routines in order, slowly at first. Then Olivia gave them a few notes and had them perform the cheers up to speed, just the way they would at Lembrook.

They were all breathing hard as they collapsed around the floor. Olivia was the only one who looked like she was ready to go again. "Well?" she demanded of their audience.

Pres made a face. "It looks too hard," he complained.

"Man, it *is* hard!" Sean exploded. He was dripping wet, his chestnut hair curling down on his forehead.

125

"But it has to seem effortless," Mary Ellen said. "The lifts, especially. You girls don't look like they're any fun."

"That's because Slammer's always calling them the 'old heave-ho,'" Hope muttered.

"And Jessica," Mary Ellen went on, "you really could be quicker on all your turns."

"I know," Jessica acknowledged. She didn't want to say that the reason she was so slow was that every time she turned, she saw Patrick standing there, watching her.

"And the transitions," Pres said. "They're wobbly, like you guys really aren't sure what you're going to do next."

"That's because Slammer keeps yelling orders in the middle of the cheers, and we lose our places," Tara told him.

"But he's not here now," Olivia pointed out. "We're behaving like he's still breathing down our necks, right? Let's try the moves like we never did them before. As a matter of fact," she said, "let's do them without cheers at all. Just pure movement."

She got them in place again and Jessica reached over to turn on the recorder. But Patrick had beat her to it. Their hands touched and quickly parted. Jessica's fingers seemed to bear the imprint of Patrick's for the next hour.

The cheerleaders moved around the room, performing with concentrated ease. It did make a difference not having to speak at the same time. Even "Sharp" seemed to flow when done silently. Then they sat down and just rehearsed the words, over and over, getting the intonation just right.

Then they went back to the silent treatment.

After working through the four routines several times this way, Olivia gave them a break. And Pres, Mary Ellen, and Patrick gave them a round of applause.

"You're looking much better," Mary Ellen told Tara as they went over to the bar at the back of the rec room for some apple juice.

"Thanks," the other girl smiled. "That means a lot, coming from you." She shook her long red hair off her neck, trying to cool herself off a bit.

Mary Ellen shrugged. "Just trying to be helpful."

"I think it's great that a real New York model would even take the time to come and look at our podunk group," Tara said. "You know, I haven't really had a chance to talk to you since you got to town, but I think we have a lot in common. I want to be an actress," she confided softly.

"Oh?" Mary Ellen smiled politely, and changed the subject. "Livvy had a really good idea there. Now, when you put the words back with the cheers, they'll really fit."

"Tell me about making it," Tara begged. "I've always thought I could do it, too. You know, just do commercials and live off those until some juicy Broadway part came along. What do you think?"

The girl was so naive, and reminded Mary Ellen too much of herself. Sometimes, even she still had those dreams.

"Well, I think . . . I think you have to be realistic. If you really want to get started in the big city, you need more than luck or talent. You need

127

to be the kind of person who can hear the word 'no' over and over and not get discouraged. Commercials aren't that easy to get. You may have to start off waiting tables or working in an office. And you may have to do that in between acting jobs for a real long time."

Tara looked at her quizzically, wanting to ask some more questions, but Olivia was lining them up to start again. And as Tara threw herself back into the rehearsal, she wondered about Mary Ellen's warning. Couldn't you get everything you dreamed of if you wanted it badly enough? That was what she'd grown up thinking, and until she was proven wrong, she'd keep on believing it.

But as she went through the routines again and again, the vision of an acting career faded temporarily. What she was doing — what they were all doing — demanded full and complete attention. The jumps, the slides, the catches in midair were all starting to come together.

By nine P.M. the group was tired but hopeful. Olivia kept at it, kept trying things different ways, emphasizing different parts of the cheers. By ten, they all knew it was working. They were elated, jubilant.

"Just mark time at practice tomorrow," Olivia suggested. "Slammer will be mad enough to spit, but ignore him. And tomorrow night, we'll put on the final touches. Thanks, Pres, Melon. We needed you."

"We didn't do a thing," Pres laughed.

"We were just here," Mary Ellen pointed out.

"Exactly." Olivia smiled.

The group all gathered up their possessions and slogged to the door. Their arms and legs throbbed with the effort of working so hard, but their hearts were light. They were going to make it. At the very least, they could place.

Jessica asked Peter for a ride and walked slowly to the door behind him, using his tall, lanky body as a buffer. But Patrick was standing at the top of the stairs, and wouldn't let her pass.

"Good-night, Jessica," he said.

"Good-night." The softness in her expression said she might be ready to listen.

"We won't be able to make it over here tomorrow night. Pres and I are moving some sets and furniture for the drama department. But I want to get things straight with you," he began.

"I don't know, Patrick. When we talk, it seems to go nowhere." But she wanted desperately to make up with him.

"Will you listen at least? Just give me a little time," he said softly.

"All right," she agreed. "I need time, too." And then she felt better. Suddenly, the knot around her heart had loosened.

But her face changed again as Mary Ellen came up behind them, and they fell silent at once. Patrick walked out quickly, so that the two girls were left alone, face to face.

"After you," Jessica said politely, her voice shaking a little.

"No," Mary Ellen told her. "I'm after you, now. And the sooner you realize that, the happier you'll be." She vanished out the door, leaving Jessica sad and sorry — and still doubtful.

CHAPTER 11

"Kids, it's already four o'clock. Will you put on a little speed?" Slammer yelled at the top of his lungs as he marched down the left aisle of Tarenton High auditorium. This was not so much for the benefit of the cheerleaders, who were right behind him, but for the hoard of students milling around on the stage moving sets and props for the school play, which was the following week.

"Hey! Hey, you!" he called. He was now right in front of the orchestra pit. "Who's in charge here?" he demanded of a tiny raven-haired girl wearing a sarong, who was struggling to carry a giant fake boulder across the stage past a collection of open paint cans.

"Well," she gasped, "ah, I don't think anybody. Mrs. Lilliom left early today — she's our advisor."

"We have the stage now," Slammer informed her. "We're the cheerleaders."

A couple of boys who were hoisting a red platform snickered. "Yeah, I could have spotted cheerleaders at twenty paces," one smirked.

"Why don't we just go away?" Olivia asked wearily.

"It's not going to do us that much good to have a dress rehearsal," Tara nodded. "We were great last night at my house."

"Of course, Slammer doesn't know that," Sean pointed out.

Hope jumped down into the orchestra pit and spoke to a couple of people. She looked at the others and threw up her hands. "They say they're scheduled for this space till six. And they still have sets to paint and flats to put together."

"Slammer," Tara suggested calmly, "why don't we go back to the gym. We don't really need — "

"Of course you do!" he boomed. "I want you to have the exact conditions you're going to have tomorrow. A stage, and a lot of rows of seats ahead of you. You guys have to project all the way to the back of the house with bright lights shining in your eyes. Which means you need to practice *here*."

Slammer strode up on the stage and blew the whistle around his neck. Everything stopped.

"He would have to make a spectacle of us, wouldn't he?" Jessica whispered miserably to Peter. "He couldn't just ask them nicely to leave."

As they were standing there, wondering what to do, an eight-foot-tall brown box moved in from stage left. When the setpiece was put in place, Pres and Patrick emerged from behind it.

"Hey," Olivia called up to them. "Hi!"

"Well, hello!" Pres grinned, whipping off the length of nylon rope that been supporting the weight. He coiled it expertly around one arm, then hung it off the hook on his trucker's belt.

"You!" Slammer pointed at Patrick and Pres. "You two stick around. You know how to work lights?"

Patrick nodded, although he wasn't paying much attention. He was busy searching the house for Jessica.

"Sure, we'll help out," Pres agreed.

"Well, what are you waiting for?" Slammer asked him. "Move all this stuff backstage again. Everything."

Pres sighed and took the rope off his belt again. "I guess that means hoisting this hundred pounds again. Patrick, get the dolly — it'll take less time. Let's put all the other furniture back in the shop, behind that metal door. And get me a new rope, would you? This one's had about all the pressure it can take."

Slammer was still yelling. "I want the stage cleared off in ten. Do you read me?" he announced to the group.

The drama kids were too dumbfounded to laugh at him. A few of them went into a huddle. Slammer was obviously a faculty member, which meant that his wishes overrode theirs. "Okay, mister," one tall boy, with a mass of hair that curled to his shoulders, said at last. "But you're in *our* territory. C'mon, kids. Let's make way for the rah-rah contingent. The *cheerleaders* need a place to play."

"All you acting types, out!" Slammer yelled. "You're wearing down my kids' morale! And get the sets and the rest of that junk out of here."

Pres and Patrick scrambled around, moving the scenery offstage left, hauling paint cans, turpentine, and the paint-stained tarp off right. Then Pres went back into the shop to make space for all the junk he had to reposition, while Patrick took his place at the light board, dimmed the house lights, and snapped the master switch on. The stage was flooded with light. Then he jumped down, into the orchestra pit.

"Jessica! You've got the tape recorder, right?" Slammer called to her. "Olivia, let's go over those notes one more time. Tara, Hope, get down and do some stretches. Guys, a couple of sets of push-ups, okay?"

Jessica ran around and took the three side steps to the stage-left area where she put the tape recorder on the property table beside the light board. She rewound the tape to the beginning and turned it off, then took out the red bandanna she had in her pocket and tied it around her forehead. She started to limber up, lightly holding the edge of the front curtain as she did her leg lifts.

"Feel prepared for tomorrow?" a voice behind her asked.

She whipped around to see Patrick standing beside her, uncoiling a new rope.

"Sort of. A lot depends on how everybody feels."

"I know what you mean." He took a pack of matches from his jeans pocket and lit one, singeing the end of the rope so that it wouldn't unravel. Then he shook out the match and deposited it in a half-empty soda can that someone had left on the prop table. "I'm coming to take some pictures . . . and to root for you," he said simply. "If you want a ride or anything, I'll be leaving early."

"Oh, that's okay," she answered. "I mean, I would, except Slammer's taking us in his van."

"I see."

"Hey!" Slammer was suddenly on top of them. "Didn't you hear me? I said turn the recorder on. They're all in position. And you" — he nodded to Patrick — "give me lights across the front of the house, and turn 'em up bright."

Jessica snapped the machine on and ran to join the other cheerleaders, wondering why it was so difficult for her just to accept what Patrick had to offer. He was so eager to make up, and she kept putting him off. Was she doing it just to be difficult? she wondered. Or did she really want to make him miserable until Mary Ellen was safely out of town? That wasn't like her at all.

In a half daze, she moved through the first obligatory cheer. It was a practice piece that all the teams had been given, to show off the basics: cartwheels, rolls, back flips, splits, and a variety of different jumps. Olivia had drilled them on it hard the past three nights at Tara's house, but she had also added some head turns and hand gestures that made it a little fancier — and made it something of their own.

By the time they got to the "Pride" cheer, they were all really excited. The music was right, the lifts were perfect, even the lilt in their voices sounded good. They went right on to Holly's jazz number, and although it had given them a little trouble the previous night, today the syncopation was perfect. As for "Sharp," it was crisp and neat — a little slower than usual, but really fine.

"Whew. I don't believe it," Slammer said when they'd finished. He walked up the aisle, crossing the wooden plank that temporarily connected the orchestra pit with the stage. "You're not as bad as you were last week."

Jessica smiled at Tara, Olivia nudged Sean in the ribs, and Hope gave Peter's hand a squeeze. There was no doubt about it — they were good. Slammer would never admit it, but they were.

"Let me tell you, all four of your routines could stand improvement," Slammer went on. "I have a lot of notes, particularly on your jazz number, but I need a second to get organized. All right, break time. See you in fifteen." He vanished offstage right, fumbling in his pockets for something, and the kids quickly dispersed.

"I guess we didn't impress him," Sean said to Pres, who had come back down into the house in time to see the last cheer. He magically made a soda materialize from out of his toolbox.

"It doesn't matter." Patrick grinned at them, his hands on his hips. He walked right over to Jessica, whose skin was flushed from exercise, and from the sight of him so near. "It looks like that hard work paid off," he told the group, but he was looking straight at Jessica.

"Now all we have to do is keep it up," Olivia said. "And hope that the St. Cloud team is having a bad day."

"Or a coach like Slammer," Sean smirked.

"Stop hoarding that soda, will you?" Pres demanded, grabbing it from him. "There are a few other people here who deserve — " He stopped as he saw the door to the auditorium open and close. A tall, slim blonde carrying a suitcase started down the right aisle toward them. The lights were shining in his eyes, but he would have known that graceful, assured gait anywhere.

"Melon!" He ran to her, a strange, panicky feeling in the pit of his stomach.

"Oh, Pres, you'll never believe it!" She was so excited, and so beautiful, and he knew from the expression on her face that she was leaving.

"What?" he demanded. "What's with the suitcase?"

"I'm on my way to the airport."

"You said you'd stay another week," he reminded her. "We have so much to — "

"I know, but Pres, I can't turn down an offer like this. There was a message for me on our answering machine, and Bonnie called to tell me. This agency, well, I've been trying to get in with them for months, and they finally called with a commercial audition." She stopped when she saw what it was doing to him. "Oh, Pres, I'm sorry — *honest* — but I have to go. They want to see me tomorrow, first thing."

He'd been meaning to talk to her about the future — and now it was too late. She would fly back to New York and get all wrapped up in her work, and who knew when she'd be in Tarenton again.

"Well, I guess I have no choice except to ask

my boss for some time off so I can take a trip to the big city. Would you let me sleep on the couch?" he said, trying to keep it light.

"Silly. *I* sleep on the couch. But we'll find a place for you." She took his hand, and he clasped hers in both of his. He was so dear to her, and she was going to miss him so terribly.

"Mary Ellen, listen to me. I want you . . . I . . . I'm the kid with the quick line, and I can't get two words out. We have some really important things to talk about."

She put a finger to his lips. "Shh. Not now. We can't now."

She felt so much, so quickly. Since leaving her hometown, she had made it an unspoken rule not to let her personal life interfere with her plans, because she had so much at stake. But she had discovered something about herself and about Pres Tilford in the past two weeks. They might be from different worlds, they might live thousands of miles apart, but there was something strong between them.

As she gazed into his eyes, she felt a longing for a life she had never considered. For the first time, she thought it just might be possible to be a model, and a success, and a person in love, too. It was worth a try. "Pres," she said softly, putting her arms around his neck, "Come see me soon."

"I think I love you," he responded, and suddenly, they were in each other's arms, holding on for dear life. Their kiss was deep and passionate, a promise between them.

Slowly, regretfully, they drew apart. The sounds of activity onstage brought them back to the everyday world they had left for a few moments. "I . . . I guess I have to get back. I said I'd help," he told her.

"Never mind. My father's bus passes here at five-thirty. He'll drop me at the airport. You have my number," she said as she picked up her suitcase and began backing up the aisle.

"I'll call you," he said.

"Tell the others to be fantastic tomorrow. Tell them I'll be thinking of them. I don't really want to say good-bye — you understand."

"Okay."

She was at the door now, and she took one last look at him before she turned. She wanted to remember him, just like that, that look of love on his face. But she *had* to leave.

"This isn't the end, Melon," he whispered under his breath. He walked back down the aisle, then turned and jumped up onto the bridge over the orchestra pit. He was filled with sadness and joy, and a kind of anticipation he had never known before.

"Oh, there you are," Patrick commented.

"What next?" Pres asked, but he wasn't talking about moving furniture, and Patrick knew it.

"Did she leave?" Patrick wanted to know.

Pres nodded.

"Tough luck. She'll be back, I bet."

This time Pres shrugged. Patrick was the one person he couldn't discuss it with. "Look, there's plenty for us to finish up in the shop while these guys get through the rehearsal. Let's get a few ropes and tackle the big pieces." He jumped onto the stage, just skirting Slammer, who was coming back from the offstage right wing.

"Remember to close that metal door, would you?" Patrick called to him. He picked up a dolly and lugged it behind him, only half-hearing the criticism that Slammer had started to give the cheerleaders.

"You can't tell me 'Sharp' is fast enough that third time through," Slammer was saying to Olivia. "You barely kept up with the tape recorder. Jessica, get back up there and turn it on. Tara, Sean, go up with her. I want to see you do that quick switch at the end."

"But we told you, if we pick up too much speed, the last lift looks rushed," Olivia explained.

The music blared from the wings, covering Slammer's answer. Tara and Sean went into their positions, marking the point in the cheer that the coach wanted to see again.

Sean gave Tara his hand to start the lift. "What's that smell? Don't you smell smoke?" he asked, but she couldn't hear him because she was now upside down, her long red hair sweeping the floor.

"Try it again!" Slammer called. "Stop the music! Go back!"

Jessica felt her eyes burning. She blinked, then took the bandanna off her sweaty forehead as she flicked the switch on the recorder and rewound it. The man was impossible. At this rate, they'd never get home in time for dinner.

She didn't know how right she was.

CHAPTER

Hot ashes, scattered on the drop cloth under the flats offstage right, hit the two turpentine-soaked cleanup rags beside the open paint can. The potent fumes ignited, and the rags caught quickly.

Within seconds, the floor seethed with fire. The flames crawled toward the heating ducts and the forced air fanned them taller and hotter. They licked at the flat piece of scenery, then traveled across it, eating the glue and linen, the light plywood frame. The hot breath of the fire blew on the first stage curtain, and it caught.

The connecting wall between the stage and the costume room was only made of flimsy partition board. The fire gobbled it up greedily, swallowing the dresses, pants, hats, and shoes in moments. Then it pushed on through into the prop room, where it devoured the assortment of items for the show. It was moving rapidly now, demanding more fuel.

From the shop, behind the metal door, it was difficult to smell anything onstage except the pervasive odor of paint and glue, but Patrick was aware of something different, an acrid smell that caused his eyes to burn and tear.

"You smell something?" he asked Pres.

"Huh? Not me." Pres was busy strapping the heavy bureau to his back.

"Take over a sec. I want to check this out," Patrick insisted.

"Don't run out on me now, pal. I'll get a hernia," Pres protested, but Patrick was already gone.

He ran to the metal door that separated the shop from the backstage area. It was closed, as it usually was, to muffle the sound for the performers. As he put his hand on it, he leaped back with a shout of pain. It was red hot. Ripping up a piece of carpet from the floor, he covered his knuckles for protection from the heat.

"Pres! Help! There's a fire." Patrick raced to the alarm box in the hallway and cracked the glass. The alarm rang out.

In the house, Hope, Peter, and Olivia leaped up as smoke billowed out across the stage. "Get off the stage!" Olivia yelled to Tara and Sean. They looked confused, both of them whipping around toward the sight of the curtain roaring up in flames.

"Jessica!" Tara called. Sean started toward the left wing and Tara grabbed his hand. They couldn't see or hear the kids in the auditorium now. They were alone on a terrifying island, with danger at every turn.

Hope ran up the right aisle of the auditorium with Peter right behind her. "I'll get the alarm," she said. Then she heard its peal, and realized that someone — probably the guys in the shop — had beaten her to it. That meant that *they* were okay, at least.

Hope and Peter reached the door right after Slammer, who was yelling orders to no one in particular. Olivia started to follow them, but she turned toward the stage as the sprinkler system went on, and she felt drops of water pelting her head. "It's not enough!" she cried as she saw the second curtain burst into flame. She couldn't see if all of them were up there. Jessica was stage left — was she all right?

On the other side of the fire, Patrick yanked at the metal door. Pres pulled him back forcibly. "Don't do that! You don't want it spreading in here! Once those metal doors are open, we're in trouble."

"But Jessica's out there. And Tara and Sean. Where's Slammer?" he demanded. "We can't just leave those kids."

"Let it go, Patrick!" Pres wrenched him away, but not soon enough. Patrick jerked the door with all his strength.

Jessica was the last to realize what was going on. By the time she saw the fire on the other side of the stage, it was too late. She was surrounded by smoke, unable to see a thing in front of her or behind her. She tried to calm herself, and decided to stay put and wait for help to come. If she started walking, she might inadvertently go toward the flames instead of away from them.

The fire spread around the back of the stage and into the shop with a horrible sucking noise, leaping through the open door and consuming the floor nearby, growing redder and wilder as it was fed by the heavy backstage curtains. Sean and Tara recoiled from it in horror.

"Where's Jessica?" Tara gasped, clinging to Sean's hand for dear life.

"Jessica, follow the sound of my voice!" Sean yelled.

She heard him, but she was confused, unable to figure out directions in the midst of all the smoke.

Tara let go of Sean and started moving. "I can just make her out — see, she's over there. Jessica!" And then a plume of charcoal smoke obscured her view. She couldn't see Jessica anymore, but she darted out into the stage-left area before Sean could stop her.

"Tara, get back here!" Sean yelled. But she didn't answer.

Patrick, with Pres right behind him, came charging through the door to the stage, accidentally hitting Sean and shoving him to his knees. Pres bent down to help him up.

"What's going on? Where's Jessica?" Patrick demanded.

"I don't know, man. Tara went over there." He pointed vaguely. "I told her not to." He squinted, then covered his eyes with his hand. The heat was intolerable now, the smoke a noxious, searing pain that entered his lungs and chest, holding him captive. He dropped down on the floor and started to crawl.

Jessica couldn't hear their voices anymore. It seemed so dark all of a sudden, and she was terrified. She couldn't breathe — only pant — and that scared her. Maybe it would be safer to get away from the curtains.

Heat rises. She remembered that much from sixth-grade science class. So she ducked down near the floor and began to inch her way forward. She found herself touching something smooth and hot, and although it hurt, she made herself feel its contours so that she could determine where she was. What landmark was this? Of course, it was the water cooler at the back of the stage! She whipped the bandanna out of her pocket and, burning her hand on the scorching metal, she lifted herself up, leaning on the spigot with a prayer that it still functioned. The cooler sent a flow of uncomfortably hot water onto the red cloth. She gasped, but pressed it to her face. It was better than nothing.

Sean didn't know where he was, but he sensed Pres and Patrick close by. The fire was louder now.

Pres covered his ears to block off the painful heat. "C'mon, you two, the orchestra pit's over there. It's lower than the fire. And once we get down there, I know where to look for the exit sign."

He was only grateful that Mary Ellen was gone. Now he had just one thought — to survive. He felt his way, coughing and choking, hoping that he was right about that red glow high above him on the opposite wall. If he still had his directions straight, that was the emergency exit that opened right onto the parking lot.

He threw himself forward, forcing another mouthful of smoke down. He was nauseated now, but that was nothing compared to the feeling that his lungs were about to burst. He kept reaching ahead of him, feeling for the lip of the stage. And then, just when he thought he'd been dreaming, he caught hold of it.

He did a forward roll, feeling the hard floor rush up to greet him. From there, it was only a few steps to the door. He put his weight into it, willing the door to open. It did.

The air that rushed into the auditorium was blissfully cool against his skin. But where was Jessica? And Tara? "This way, Patrick! Sean!" he called.

At that moment, Jessica was crawling along the side of the stage. She didn't know how much longer she could take the heat. She had been holding her breath, but as she moved another step forward, she knew she had to let the air out and take more in. And then, right beside her, another curtain caught. The power of the fire that reared up beside her knocked her over, the brightness of the flames blinding her. When she let the next breath flood her lungs, it was almost too much for her. She lay there immobile, unable to go on.

Patrick swung himself out through the exit door right after Pres. The two of them made it outside in time to hear the sound of a fire engine's whine, coming closer. Then a second siren, and a third.

Patrick looked at Pres, and for a moment,

he didn't recognize him. His friend's face was black with soot. "Where's Sean?" he gasped. "I thought he was right behind us."

Five engines converged on the school at once, and firemen began hauling their hoses out. The largest truck raised its cherry-picker arm and a battery of men scrambled up the ladder to begin directing streams of water from above. Three men pointed hoses at the auditorium windows, and a separate unit ran around the side of the school to get at the shop.

Just below the far window, Tara inched along the floor. She didn't think she had any strength left in her, but she was determined to get out. She moved on, not knowing that she was moving away from the lip of the stage and the exit door. She felt confused and lightheaded from all the smoke she'd breathed.

At last she struggled to her knees, then got into a crouch, looking up to try to get a sense of where she was. With her next step, she tripped and went sprawling. Then the air cleared for a moment and she saw the familiar face. It was Sean. She crawled toward him, barely reaching him before she passed out in his arms.

"Come on. You've got to get up," he hollered in her ear. He coughed, gathering her slight body to him.

As he struggled to his feet, holding her close, he saw Jessica. She was right ahead of them, her hands feeling the air in front of her. She reached them and curled into a ball, trying to shield her body from the heat.

"We're going to be all right," Jessica murmured, more to herself than to the other two. They were fine, now that they were together again. They had to be.

"Help me with her," Sean gasped. He draped one of Tara's arms around Jessica's neck and put the other around his own, tensing the limp body against his. She was a small girl, always light on her feet, but right now she was dead weight, and Jessica wasn't helping. Sean felt like he was carrying both of them, as he grunted and moved forward. The orchestra pit was somewhere around here.

"Open your eyes, would you!" he begged, but Tara didn't respond. And Jessica seemed to be getting weaker by the minute.

"C'mon, Jessica. Just another minute and we're clear."

"I can't," she sobbed. "I'm sorry." She let go and knelt on the floor.

They were so close now, he could feel it. He put Tara back down on the floor and grabbed her under both arms, then directed Jessica to take Tara's feet and crawl along after them. Slowly, very slowly, he began to drag Tara. He had his back to the worst of the fire, and he felt better for a moment, not quite so disoriented. He kept moving with her, one step at a time, for what seemed an eternity. And then he felt the lip of the stage.

"Jump down, Jessica!" he ordered her. "The exit door's just behind you."

She did as he told her, and he saw her vanish through the door. Then he gathered Tara in his arms and jumped with her, landing hard on his knee. The intense pain that shot through him was welcome. They were safe. They were going to make it. He took her under the arms again and dragged her to the door. The door to freedom.

Pres and Patrick, surrounded by firemen and paramedics in the parking lot, were frantic. "There are three people left in there!" Patrick shouted at the fire chief, Captain Browning.

"We're going in after them, don't worry," the man responded. "Hawkins, follow me," he said to his deputy. "Stay close. Come on, you six." He pointed to the men he wanted with him. "But the minute I turn around and run for the door, you do the same. I don't want any heroes, understand! Let's go!"

The firemen, their oxygen masks in place, raced inside the burning building. The back stairwell, an enclosed shaft of concrete, was the only access. The men got up to the first level and chopped open the door to the auditorium. The fierce flames held them back, beating against them like waves.

The chief rushed in, staying low. The other men went in several yards further, reaching the exit door at the same time as Sean, Tara, and Jessica.

"Give her to me," Captain Browning ordered when he saw Tara. "Can you walk?"

Sean nodded. "I'm okay."

"Is there anyone else?" the chief yelled to Sean. He shook his head.

The firemen were back outside in no time, hustling their charges to safety. Captain Browning yanked off his helmet, shaking his head as he looked up toward the windows that still belched flames, despite the force of the water from the hoses. "You kids were lucky. Luckier 'n that."

A second battalion of firemen quickly rushed into the building, sending streams of water before them. The waiting ambulance squad raced with stretchers to the kids, but Patrick refused to lie down on one. He had been about to run back into the building himself, when he saw Jessica stagger out. And then he felt tears come to his eyes.

"Jessica!" He embraced her and she crumpled against his chest. "Are you all right?"

She could only nod. She hadn't the strength to say a word.

The paramedics had Tara on a stretcher with an oxygen mask over her face before Sean could even tell them she was in trouble. Then they made him lie down, and Jessica, too, while they checked them for smoke inhalation. They lay silent, slowly taking deep breaths of the precious fresh air.

Olivia, Hope, and Peter forced their way through the barrier the police had set up as soon as they saw their friends brought out, and raced over to the stretchers. They were all talking at once when a squad car screeched to a halt beside the ambulance, and Mrs. Oetjen and the Tarenton police chief, John Foster, got out.

The principal was white-faced as she looked at the eight young people. She took Olivia by a shoulder and gazed at her sternly. "I can't tell you how worried I was when I heard. How are you all?"

"Everybody's fine. Tara passed out and Sean bruised his knee, but they're in good hands,"

Olivia explained. "Pres and Patrick got to the alarm box right in time."

The last rolling clouds of deep gray smoke rose from Tarenton High, which was now drenched, inside and out. One wall was badly scorched, but the fire was out.

"How did it start?" Mrs. Oetjen demanded. "Who saw it? Where's your supervisor? Wasn't Slammer Akins running a dress rehearsal in the auditorium tonight?"

"I'd like to ask a few questions, Mrs. Oetjen," Police Chief Foster interrupted. But before he could continue, the fire chief, Captain Browning, came over. Slammer Akins, looking shaken, was right beside him.

"Well, ma'am," Captain Browning said. "Everything's under control. You got a great old building there. A good thing, too — they don't build 'em that sturdy these days. And you got some very brave kids. As to the cause of the fire, it wasn't electrical, that's all I can say. We'd like to investigate now, see what we can find in there. Anybody got any information for me?"

Slammer was glaring at the group. His gaze traveled over the cheerleaders, the injured and the well, and came to rest on Patrick and Pres. "If you'll excuse me, Mrs. Oetjen, gentlemen, I think it's a little suspicious that these two just walked out of the fire with no trouble. I saw both of them handling matches today, I'd like to ask them to turn out their pockets."

"I know these boys, Captain Browning," Mrs. Oetjen said quickly. "And there's no cause to believe that — "

150

"Ask them to do it," Slammer insisted. "I want to see what they're carrying."

Jessica lifted her head from the stretcher. She felt foggy and dazed.

"This is dumb," Pres said, pulling at his jeans pockets. Patrick had already laid his wallet, a comb, a collection of receipts, and three ten-penny nails in front of the chief. Then he brought out a Swiss army knife and a pack of matches. Pres had matches, too.

"I think you'll agree this is suspicious," Slammer said.

"Look, we use matches to sear nylon rope. That's why we carry them," Patrick told him.

"A little carelessness is all it takes," Captain Browning said, giving both boys a penetrating look.

"I need to talk to you two," Mrs. Oetjen interjected. "Is it all right if we go inside to my office now, Chief?"

The police chief shook his head, giving Pres and Patrick a scathing look. "This isn't a school matter, Mrs. Oetjen. These boys have graduated, if I recall correctly. I'm not saying I think the fire was intentional, and I'm not saying they caused it, but we ought to investigate further. I'm going to have to bring them in."

"No!" Jessica cried, but the police chief paid no attention to her. Slammer, Mrs. Oetjen, and Chief Foster were already marching the boys past the barricade, toward the squad car. The cheerleaders looked on in shocked horror as Pres and Patrick were ushered inside. The car door locked behind them.

151

CHAPTER

"This is outrageous!" Jessica jumped up shakily to go after the moving squad car. When Peter put a calming hand on her shoulder, she shook it off angrily. "Don't you realize what's going on here?" she demanded of the others, whirling around. "They're about to railroad those two boys for something they didn't do."

Olivia rubbed her forehead thoughtfully. "If there was only some way to prove that."

"They *would* have to have been carrying matches," Sean muttered. He had gotten off his stretcher when he heard the squad car approach, and although his knee smarted a little, it wasn't important now.

"But lots of people carry matches," Hope said. "Everybody who smokes cigarettes, for instance. I think — "

"But that's it!" Jessica cried, her worried expression dissolving. She lunged at Hope and hugged her tightly around the neck. "Oh, thank you! You're brilliant, Hope! I'll bet anything that's it. I never would have thought of it until it was too late. Peter, c'mon. We're going over to the station. Well, what's everybody standing around for? Let's go."

"Would you mind telling us what's going on?" Sean demanded.

"No time. Look, Tara will be okay here. They probably want to get her over to the hospital just to check her out," Jessica told him, starting for Peter's car.

Sean shook his head, looking down at the white face of the girl he had carried from the burning building. Just the sight of her, so weak and pale, lying there helpless before him, erased all the annoyance he'd ever felt toward her. And as long as she promised never to look at Ray Elliott again, he would be the first to apologize — and to let her know how much he really cared. He wanted to be there to tell her that, as soon as she came around. "I'll stay with her. But I want to know what's going on!" he yelled after them as the other four went running.

Jessica refused to explain anything in the car on the way over to the police station. She said that she needed to think. But she assured them that she was absolutely positive Pres and Patrick were not in any way responsible for the fire.

She was out of the car even before Peter pulled into an available visitor's parking space. As she ran up the steps, she had a vivid picture of Patrick being fingerprinted and having his mug shot taken, then being thrown into the holding pen with a lot of unsavory characters. It was like one of those TV shows, where the cops pin the crime on the wrong man, who has to spend the rest of his life appealing his case.

They'd let Patrick make just one phone call. He didn't know any lawyers, as far as she recalled, so he'd have to call his father, who would get totally hysterical when he heard his son had been arrested. Suppose this went on Patrick's permanent record? What would happen to the trash business and the moving business with Pres? They might completely dissolve the second one. They'd probably take away Patrick's driver's license, too, and he'd never be able to get a good job — not be mention the fact that he'd be emotionally scarred for life.

Oh, why hadn't she been nicer to him? She'd been so rotten about Mary Ellen, and probably without cause. She was sure now that there'd been no reason to be jealous, really, but she'd made him suffer. Now, sitting alone in the holding pen, he wouldn't even be able to conjure up the image of his girl friend's loving face, because she hadn't been awfully loving lately.

"Where's Patrick Henley?" she demanded of the cop on duty at the front desk. "And Pres Tilford?"

Olivia, Hope, and Peter were right behind her, even though Jessica was unaware of them until Olivia took her hand and urged her to stay cool.

"Oh, the two kids who started the fire at the high school?" The desk sergeant nodded toward a closed door at the back of the station. "But you can't go in there."

"We have knowledge and proof of the real perpetrator," Jessica went on, staunchly relying on the vocabulary of television drama. That was sure to impress him!

"Well, I — " The man hesitated just for a moment, which gave Jessica the opportunity to dash toward the door, with the others behind her. They were inside the interrogation room before the policeman could stop them.

"What's this?" Police Chief Foster looked up, astonished. "Corey, I thought I told you — " He glared at the desk sergeant.

"Chief, I'm really sorry. But the girl says she knows who did it."

Jessica felt her heart pounding. Patrick and Pres were seated on one side of a long table, and Mrs. Oetjen, Slammer, the police chief, and two other men — Jessica assumed they were detectives — sat on the other side. Everyone at the table looked very grim.

"Jessica, please, all of you, come sit down," Mrs. Oetjen said. "John, I hope you don't mind, but these kids are very close to one another, and they were present this afternoon when the fire broke out. I think it might be worth our while to listen to them. We should get all the information available."

The chief nodded his consent, and the cheerleaders took seats beside the two in custody. Jessica squeezed Patrick's hand. "Don't worry," she muttered under her breath.

"Okay, kids," one of the detectives grunted. "Let's hear it."

Jessica took a deep breath and cleared her

throat. "All you have on Pres and Patrick is the fact that both were carrying matches — "

" — and used them," Slammer interrupted. "I saw both of them them singe the ends of some rope this afternoon up on that stage."

Jessica gave him a small smile. "I saw that, too, coach, and I also saw them dispose of the matches. Patrick put his in a soda can — that might still be around backstage right — and Pres threw his in a bucket of water that was next to some of the paint cans when we first walked in."

"Okay," Chief Foster said in a tired voice. "If it'll make you feel better, we'll ask Captain Browning to go look for the bucket and the soda can."

Olivia and Hope exchanged glances. This wasn't any great shakes of a revelation. They didn't see how Jessica's testimony was going to save Pres and Patrick. After all, they could have lit matches at other times when she didn't see them.

"Anything else?" the chief asked. "Because if you're finished, miss, I think maybe you and your friends should be going so we can talk to the boys alone."

"I'm not finished," Jessica went on, her voice growing stronger. "It would be interesting to know if there was anyone else on that stage with matches."

"Like who?" one of the detectives wanted to know.

"Like anybody who happens to smoke cigarettes," she said, looking directly at the police chief.

"Jessica, as you know, smoking is not permitted on school property," Mrs. Oetjen said. "I don't think any of the students would risk carrying cigarettes around, knowing the consequences."

"Not a student. A teacher," Jessica stated.

There was silence in the room. Jessica waited for Slammer to speak up, but when he didn't, she stood and walked over to him. "Coach Akins, a few days ago, in your office, you told me you had one weakness. Despite your best efforts, you still smoke one cigarette a day. Isn't that true?"

Slammer's face was blank. "Oh, look," he protested, "I don't see what relevance — "

"Answer the question, Mr. Akins," the chief told him firmly.

"Sure. Yeah, I do smoke a cigarette now and again."

"Did you have one today?" Jessica asked.

He made a fist with one hand and shoved it into his palm. "You think you're so smart," he growled at her.

"Well, did you?"

"*Yes.*" The word came out like a shout.

She was about to ask another question when the door opened again and the desk sergeant, looked harried, showed the fire chief into the room.

"My people discovered something," Captain Browning told them all. "Part of a cigarette butt was found in the backstage area, near the paint and turpentine. One of the metal containers was lying on it. I guess the girl who was back there tripped and kicked it over, so the filter didn't burn up."

Jessica leaned forward toward Slammer. "When we took a fifteen minute break, you got up onstage, didn't you?"

"I remember," Patrick nodded, speaking with confidence for the first time. "It was when Mary Ellen came into the auditorium. Pres was out in the house talking to her, and the rest of you kids were sitting in the first row. When I went back to the shop to get more rope, I saw Slammer near the paint cans, backstage right."

"You got it," Slammer admitted wearily. "I needed a smoke, so I lit up behind one of the pieces of scenery where no one would see me. But I stomped the thing out!"

Captain Browning shook his head. "Looks like you didn't stomp hard enough."

"I'd like to have the evidence, if I may." The police chief held out his hand.

Slammer produced the half-empty pack of cigarettes from his back pocket and placed it carefully on the table. Tucked inside the cellophane wrapping was a pack of matches.

"Sam," Mrs. Oetjen said in a tight voice, "I find it difficult to believe that you would blatantly disregard school rules. I'm terribly upset."

"You have reason to be, Mrs. Oetjen," the fire chief nodded. "This man's mistake could have resulted in lost lives and your whole school going up in flames. Mister, if I could, I'd charge you with reckless endangerment."

"You're not going to lock me up, are you?"

158

Slammer looked panicky. "What am I gonna tell the wife?"

"There's no crime," the police chief shrugged. "You made an attempt to extinguish the cigarette — I can't even charge you with negligence. I will tell you, though, that if I ever hear anything about you again, anything at all, I'm gonna throw the book at you. And I'd suggest you kick the habit."

"Jessica, kids," Slammer extended his hands to them. "I never meant to do you any harm. I never wanted to do anything but turn you into the best cheerleading team in existence."

"Sam, you are *not* responsible for these students any longer," Mrs. Oetjen told him. "We'll just see how long Ardith Engborg is going to be laid up, and perhaps suspend cheerleading practice temporarily."

"But Mrs. Oetjen!" Olivia couldn't believe what she'd just heard. "The regionals are tomorrow in Lembrook."

"Oh, my goodness! I completely forgot," the principal exclaimed. "But you can't be in any shape to perform, after what you've been through. Tara will probably be out for a while, and — "

"Don't worry about that," Hope grinned. "I think Sean is working on her right now. I'm pretty sure Tara would want to compete tomorrow, even if she had to be carried through the whole show."

"I know she would," Olivia agreed. "We don't need a coach for tomorrow, Mrs. Oetjen. All we need is what we've got — each other."

"Well, then, it's settled." The principal nodded, getting up and ushering her students to the door. "John, you don't have to hold these two boys any longer, do you?"

The police chief gave both Pres and Patrick a hearty pat on the back. "They're free to go, with my apologies. Sorry we jumped to conclusions, boys. Mr. Akins, I'm afraid you'll have to stick around so we can get a complete statement."

Jessica couldn't say anything, her heart was so full. She just gripped Patrick's hand hard, until they were safely out the door, down the steps.

"That was terrible. I never want to go through anything like that again," she told him.

"Thanks, sweetheart." He looked down at her gratefully, linking his hands around her slim waist. "You saved me from a life behind bars," he teased.

"Don't joke about it. I imagined some pretty awful things on my way over here."

"Silly. A man is innocent until proven guilty, you know. It's the American way."

"I know that."

"Well, I *am* innocent. You just proved that. I think you ought to give me a break, too, Jessica," he said softly.

Their kiss had been a long time coming, and it was filled with trust and eagerness and a great deal of love.

"Are you two going to hang around here all night?" Pres's voice startled them out of their embrace. "Because we have a car waiting." The other cheerleaders gathered around Jessica and

160

Patrick, but the two didn't separate. They stayed together, their arms around each other.

"Peter's going to take us to the hospital to see Tara and Sean," Pres went on, "if you're interested in tagging along, that is. And then some of us better call home and inform some parents that everything's okay."

"I'll do that, Pres," Mrs. Oetjen offered. "You all go on. I can't tell you how happy I am that you're all right."

"We're in great shape," Olivia assured her. "Now that *we're* taking over."

They piled into Peter's car and started off down the street. The scorched fire smell still clung to Jessica, Patrick, and Pres, and it was a reminder of what they'd been through that day.

"Too bad we ever met that guy," Patrick said suddenly.

"I don't have a lot of pity for him," Pres commented sourly.

"I think he's just misguided," Jessica nodded. "Who knows, with a little help, he may actually turn out all right."

"You're kidding," Olivia scoffed. "Slammer Akins is a bully and a dictator. He doesn't understand people and he never will."

"Well, he'll never darken *our* door again," Hope said.

"The important thing is, he didn't hold us back," Peter pointed out. "I feel pretty good about that."

"I'll feel even better tomorrow," Jessica said. "After we win."

The others agreed completely.

CHAPTER

"And now, ladies and gentlemen, from St. Cloud Prep, the cheerleading squad known as the Angels! Give 'em a hand, folks!" The master of ceremonies, a local radio disk jockey, led the crowd in a rousing round of applause.

Olivia stood backstage, right near the curtain, where she'd been for the past twenty minutes watching the different groups perform. None of them were up to Tarenton standards, but the worst was yet to come. Or rather, the best — St. Cloud Prep.

She kept smoothing her hair back from her forehead and wrapping the little tendrils in front of her ears around her fingers. She knew she looked fine, she knew there was nothing more she could do, and yet, she had this anxious feeling in the pit of her stomach that there was just one little thing out of place.

"How do I look?" Tara whispered, adjusting

the knife pleats on her red and white skirt. She was standing with one leg raised high on top of a piano, bending her head to her knee. As she glanced up, the St. Cloud team came running past them in their blue and gold uniforms. The six girls and two boys of the competition seemed infuriatingly pleased with themselves.

"You look okay," Olivia answered, her eyes on the stage.

"Just okay?" Tara was indignant. "I nearly succumbed to smoke for the sake of the team, I still feel dizzy every once in a while, and you tell me I look *okay*?"

"You look gorgeous," Sean informed her, coming up behind them. "Never more beautiful and talented than right now."

Tara gave him a smile. "You actually sound sincere," she laughed.

"And you know what else?" Sean grinned. "I think you're *interesting*, too. Any girl who could walk out of a fire and do a cheering meet the very next day has got to be an exceptional person."

Tara was flattered, but more, she was beginning to see that Sean was a guy worth holding on to. Had Ray Elliott even called her last night to see how she was? He had not, whereas Sean had been with her through the whole thing.

Hope, Peter, and Jessica appeared from the dressing room and joined their teammates at the curtain to watch the show.

"Look at that set of flip flops," Hope sighed, staring at the stage. "Those girls are completely in sync."

163

"True, but I don't like the way that guy on the left did those handsprings," Peter commented.

"Will you all stop talking and do some breathing?" Olivia said nervously. "We shouldn't even be watching the others. It's only going to throw us off. Is everybody warmed up?"

The kids nodded, their eyes still riveted on the excellent performance of the St. Cloud cheerleaders. They finished their first routine, and the crowd went wild.

"Oh, dear," Hope groaned, turning away. "I can't watch anymore." She grabbed Peter's hand and slowly, he followed her to the stage door.

Olivia moved the others away before the second number started. She realized that it was important to keep their morale high, to keep them convinced that they could do anything. She reached for a few words to say to them. A pep talk, right. That was what Mrs. Engborg always gave them before a game.

"Everybody! Let's congregate over here, okay?" She walked toward the back of the stage and grouped them in a circle around her. "Now listen to me. We've had a rough time these past few weeks, and we didn't get much of a dress rehearsal."

"Guess whose fault *that* was," Sean scoffed.

"But it doesn't matter," Olivia went on. "We could have no rehearsal at all, and still do brilliantly, and you know why?"

Jessica put a hand on Olivia's shoulder. "Because we're in charge of our performance. We know just what we want to do."

"Right," Tara concurred. "I think that's the ticket to success."

"And there's something else," Olivia reminded them. "We don't have to be first to be great. Even though we probably will be," she quickly added.

A burst of wild applause from the audience made them turn toward the stage. St. Cloud was finished with their second piece.

"Maybe just a few more stretches," Olivia suggested, trying to keep her crew from wandering back to watch the performance in progress.

But at that moment, the outer door to the backstage area opened, and the cheerleaders looked in amazement at the sight before them. Pres and Patrick were pushing Ardith Engborg, seated in a wheelchair, over the cables and wires that ran around the floor. Mrs. Engborg's left leg was bound up in a huge white cast with red stripes — the Tarenton colors. She was moving toward them with her arms outstretched, a huge smile on her face.

"I don't believe it!" Jessica cried, running toward the coach and taking her hand.

"What are you doing here?" Olivia exclaimed. The team gathered around her, all talking at once, so excited and thrilled to see her they couldn't get a coherent sentence out.

"Hold on! Quiet. For heaven's sake!" Mrs. Engborg laughed.

"We pried this lady out of the hospital a day early," Pres explained. "Her doctor said she was giving orders to the nurses and causing a ruckus, so he was glad to see her go."

"Then we ran a ramp up the side of the moving truck for the chair," Patrick went on, "and lifted her into the cab and started out for Lembrook. We haven't missed anything crucial, have we?" He moved closer to Jessica so that he could give her a hug. It was almost impossible for him to see her and not touch her now.

"No, it's just St. Cloud," Hope told him.

"You notice how she says *just*." Sean smirked.

"Don't worry about them," Mrs. Engborg cautioned him. "I saw them at a game a month ago, and they simply didn't have it."

Tara shook her head, glancing back toward the stage as, once again, the applause poured forth. "That's their third routine. Sounds like the audience is eating it up."

Mrs. Engborg shook a finger in her face. "Any team who can survive Slammer Akins, plus a fire, can do anything. You remember that."

"Yeah, I guess that's true." Peter grinned. "Have you missed us?"

Mrs. Engborg's blue eyes were shining. "A little."

"What's a coach without her six red and white horses?" Sean demanded. He pawed the floor and threw his head back for a convincing neigh. "Here we are, madam, ready and willing to do your bidding."

"Then win," she said simply. "I'll be watching."

"We're right with you, guys," Pres said. "And so's Mary Ellen. I talked to her this morning," he added. The others could tell that his mind was not exactly on the regional competition, but in

166

New York, a thousand miles away.

"Be wonderful as always," Patrick counseled them. He patted the Pentax around his neck. "I'm recording you for posterity."

Then Mrs. Engborg motioned for Pres to push her back, and, as quickly as the three had appeared, they were gone again.

The St. Cloud team finished to another burst of applause. They raced offstage, but went back for three curtain calls.

"It's our turn," Olivia said in a hushed voice. She lined the kids up and, without a word, they joined their hands together, making a silent pact to be terrific.

"Our next group, the cheerleading team from Tarenton High," the disk jockey boomed through his microphone. "Let's hear it for Tarenton!"

Jessica snapped on the tape recorder and took her place in line. She was breathing hard already, and she hadn't done a thing. It was exhilaration, pure and simple. They all felt it.

The stage lights nearly blinded Olivia as she ran onstage, leading the others, but she didn't let that stop her. Her face glowed, her voice was strong, and her first cartwheel was absolute perfection. She let Sean pull her to him, and suddenly, she was up in the air, letting the cheer ring out.

This was the practice number, the one all the other teams before them had started with. The audience was bored with it by now because they had seen it six times already. But the Tarenton version was different. It had those extra added attractions that Olivia had worked so hard on.

And the judges loved it. The group finished the first cheer to a standing ovation. After that, they were sure they could do no wrong.

They swung right into the "Pride" cheer as the music changed.

"We're loud,
Hear us yell!
We're proud!
Can't you tell?"

The smiles on their six faces were for real. They were grinning like crazy because they knew they were performing at the peak of their abilities.

Jessica had purposely left space on the tape in between the second and third cheers so that they could stay in position and breathe a little before launching into the difficult jazz number. Olivia quickly looked at her teammates, checking them over. Hope and Peter were ready to go, Sean and Jessica looked prepared, but she noticed that Tara seemed to be out of breath just as the music began for the third piece.

"Give us a minute,
A minute of your time!
Let us entertain you,
We can be sublime!

We're the ones to beat,
We're the team with heat!
Look!
Out!
We're fresh!

We're bad!
We're hot!
Tarenton Wolves —
Give it all you got!"

The cheer was so well choreographed that each word was emphasized by a movement. And each cheerleader did his or her most impressive stunts in the number. Tara, who was a fantastic gymnast, had a running set of aerial flips across the floor. But as Sean gave her the boost and she started off, Olivia could tell something was wrong. Tara was off her mark, and she wasn't spotting properly. Suddenly, Olivia remembered her comment about feeling dizzy.

Tara slipped and hit hard, landing on one shoulder, but she recovered immediately, substituting a forward roll for the rest of her flips. The other cheerleaders were ready to cover for her, but it wasn't necessary. She was fine again, performing as well as she ever had.

"Can you do the last number?" Olivia mouthed to her as they finished to a round of applause. The audience didn't seem to know that anything had gone wrong.

Tara didn't waste breath talking. She just kept moving into her next position, and she nodded at her captain as the music began for "Sharp." Like a trooper, she carried through the number without a hitch, and when the group finished in splits on the floor, her head was the highest, her smile the brightest.

"Thank you, kids!" the D.J. called over the

sound of the audience. "Weren't they great, ladies and gentlemen?"

The cheerleaders lined up for their curtain call at the edge of the stage. The applause rippled through the house, and although it didn't seem as frantic as the clapping for St. Cloud, it was still pretty enthusiastic. They ran off and came back twice more to receive the approval of the audience.

"Let's go out front and watch the rest of the show," Olivia suggested.

"I'd rather jump out the window," Tara grumbled.

"Oh, stop," Sean told her. "I don't want to hear any of that." He dragged her along, behind the others, out the door and around to the back of the huge auditorium.

There were fifteen more groups after them, and as the cheerleaders sat together, critically appraising the competition, they felt good, really good. They had, in fact, done their best, and that was all that counted. When the last team had finished and the judges went into their huddle, they got up and went down the aisle toward Mrs. Engborg's wheelchair.

"You were magnificent," she said. "Nothing less."

"I messed up. How could I be so dumb!" Tara wailed.

"You were incredible," Mrs. Engborg objected. "I've never seen a recovery like that."

"They loved us," Hope assured her. "You heard them."

"But what about the judges?" Tara groaned.

"We'll just have to see," Olivia told her.

Five minutes later, the disk jockey took the stage again. He had a small white envelope in his hand. "The judges have reached their decision, folks," he said. "And a difficult one it was, too."

The crowd was suddenly hushed. The different teams, dressed in their school colors, stood in groups along the far aisles. Only the six Tarenton cheerleaders held hands. The energy they had poured into their performance now coursed back and forth among them, and they shared their hopes and anxieties as they waited for the announcement.

"In third place," the D.J. read, "the dynamic team from Braxton! In second place," he went on quickly, "Tarenton High! And our winners, the Angels of St. Cloud Prep! C'mon up here, kids!"

In a daze, the six Tarenton cheerleaders walked forward with the members of the other two teams and climbed the stairs onto the stage. They were too busy being happy to think about the fact that they hadn't placed first. The D.J. put a plaque in Olivia's shaking hands, and then arranged the three teams to accept the kudos of the audience. Each group in turn stepped forward and took a bow, and the applause didn't stop.

Finally, the D.J. waved his hands frantically and yelled into the microphone for silence. "Just a second!" Feedback whined through the house, and everybody quickly stopped talking and clapping.

"The judges tell me," he began, "that this year, we have another award — a very special one — to present. For the cheerleading squad with the most team spirit, our prize tonight goes to none other than — Tarenton High!"

Jessica wondered if she'd heard right. Tara started crying, and Sean put his arms around her. Hope and Peter were jumping up and down, and Olivia was laughing hysterically as the D.J. handed her a small bronze medal that was inscribed with one word — TEAMWORK. They took each other's hands again, and came toward the bright, welcoming stage lights and the love of the crowd.

As they bowed low once more and stepped back, they knew they had something that no other team possessed. They had each other.

Will the New Orleans Mardi Gras be too hot for the cheerleaders to handle? Read Chearleaders #27, SPRING FEVER.